Baptism for the Dead
a novel

LIBBIE HAWKER

Baptism for the Dead
Copyright 2012 – 2014, 2015, 2016
Libbie Hawker
Second Print Edition

This book is a work of fiction.
Any resemblance to actual persons, living or dead,
or to actual events, is coincidental.

Running Rabbit Press
RunningRabbitBooks.com

San Juan County, WA

Cover design and formatting
by Running Rabbit Press

For you, Bluebird.

MORE BOOKS BY LIBBIE HAKER

Arts and Crafts with Dead Animals: A Memoir
November, 2016

Tidewater
Mercer Girls
Daughter of Sand and Stone
The Sekhmet Bed
The Crook and Flail
Sovereign of Stars
The Bull of Min
House of Rejoicing
Storm in the Sky
Eater of Hearts

CONTENTS

Initiatory..... 7
Creation..... 91
Garden of Eden..... 105
The Lone and Dreary World..... 147
The Nail in the Sure Place..... 199
Veil..... 265

Initiatory

Initiatory

1.

The roads in Rexburg are too wide. Four lanes through the heart of town, rows of pale-barked trees in precise square holes that break the sidewalks at regular intervals. The sidewalks are level and straight, empty but hopeful, running neat in front of the shops that sit like abandoned cardboard boxes, dull-colored with faded signs. This Space for Lease in white shoe paint flaking off a window. A kid has scratched his initials into the opaque streaked L. These small acts of self-proclamation pass here for petty crime.

Now and then a car passes, a big one, a minivan or something more masculine but with plenty of seating for the kids, probably belonging to a chiropractor or a professor, too bright against the speechless dun of old brick facades and cinder-block walls. The few cars on the road move like prairie schooners, bold against the vastness of all that open space. Big houses in pale hues cling to the sides of every road and hold hands, red rover, red rover, and out beyond it's isolation, picked last for the team.

But the roads are the thing. Wide like flood rivers in a badland, scouring, dominating, so great that when you stand on the dry sidewalk

Baptism for the Dead

and watch the streets you can feel the burden of the dreams that built them. If you look hard enough, if the sun slants at the right angle in the afternoons when the clouds gather out west, you will see apparitions. They are the specters of the dreams that built Rexburg: ghost cars sweeping by, silent, with fender fins and wood paneling, wheels a slow-motion blur. Cars full of perfect children, moms who forgot to take their aprons off, dads with big line-art smiles and tidy fedoras, all of them transparent and color-reversed, photo negatives. You see all this, if the light hits just right, through a dissolving, particulate haze: the plans of the pioneers who plowed these roads into the ground, a dream collapsing into a final burst of scent and sound, a golden flare of light, scattering just before the dreamer wakes.

The Thirty-Three runs through town like a line sketched on a yellow canvas, glancing and fast. The highway draws out to Sugar City, out to the mysterious hot places where streams sink into the golden sighing earth and reappear where you do not expect them, out to Sugar City and on and on toward a dense purple stillness on the horizon, far away from this place.

*

Initiatory

The setting is the first thing. If you don't understand *where* you won't understand at all. Let me draw this out in a grid: a topographic map of Madison County. Rexburg, Idaho. Population 18,647. College campus on the hill. Golden brick hospital with state-of-the-art maternity center. Business establishments in order of economic importance: retail, health, real estate, agriculture. Ethnicity: white. Religion: Latter-Day Saint. Sex: male. Five-point-five children per household. White picket fence, dog in yard, pot roast with carrots and potatoes on Sundays. *Approved housing for young ladies* just off West Fourth Street. Virtually no crime or Democrats. It's the Best Place in America to Raise a Family. Nobody knows who first declared this, but everybody in town believes it with a wide-eyed, breathless sensation of good fortune, the kind that settles like a royal mantle over winners of lotteries, raffles, cake walks.

I grew up here, went to college here, was married and sealed to my husband here in the new temple on the hill. Sealed together for time and eternity.

At night the temple lights up like a pillar of fire.

2.

There are always eyes watching, day or night. This is what the eyes saw in 1999, the summer I turned fourteen.

*

They call themselves the Latter-Day Saints, and they mean it, that bit about the latter days. On the surface it's all board games and Kool-Aid, but look in the pantry of the most Norman-Rockwellian of homes and you will find stores of potable water wax-sealed in jugs, bags of popcorn seed and cans of beans, five-gallon buckets of honey with opaque crumbling crusts of crystallized sugars and drowned ants. Years' worth of goods laid away as surety against the impending Second Coming of Christ, guaranteed to happen any day now, any moment, in fact.

Not a soul in Rexburg draws breath but doesn't believe that these are the Last Days, and in 1999, when the Great Odometer of Planet Earth was about to roll over to a lot of fresh and terrifying zeros, every citizen was more certain than ever that the End Times were at hand.

Initiatory

Rexburg, of course, being thoroughly righteous through and through, would be spared – exalted, even, once God was done scouring the planet with His cleansing fire. Everyone was watchful for signs, and everything was a sign of the End: politics, routine earthquakes, lunar eclipses. I remember one dinner with extended family where my grandfather casually remarked that the President was on his way to a summit meeting somewhere far away, and one of my aunts clutched her napkin against her blouse and said fearfully, with her End Times face studied and pale and meek, "Summit meeting? That sounds *scary*." Scary meant one thing: the terrible blare of the angel's horn. The ground heaving in fear. Christ with his tongue like a sword, his eyes like fire.

Incidentally, years later I learned that the new millennium didn't technically start until January 1, 2001, and I felt vaguely cheated, like the whole gut-clenching year of '99 had been a cosmic prank. But at the time, everyone was sure the coming New Year was our big moment. Nobody could wait. Housewives chomped at their bits. Boys thrilled to the prospect of missions spent spreading the word of God in apocalyptic wastelands, where forlorn survivors of the Lord's wrath would be only too glad to be baptized. They'd need no convincing at all. It would be like Disneyland, with considerably more pestilence. Everyone in Rexburg eyed their pantry stores with jocularity. Oh, you baked beans and soggy canned asparagus. We'll soon be opening you while we watch the fireworks!

*

Everyone in Rexburg believed but two. I was one. The other was Adam. He was fourteen, just like me. It was the summer before ninth grade and very windy, and we were in love.

We met on the last day of school. The bell had just rung, and I was pedaling hard for home down a long quiet street where shade from old dry-barked trees alternated with pools of sunlight on the parched sidewalk. I didn't slow as I came to the corner; I didn't look, either. The front wheels of our bikes smashed together; we both flew to the pavement. Stunned and stinging, I picked myself up carefully, brushed grit from my tender scraped palms. Adam said "Sh–it," drawing out the sibilant with a wild acceleration, the sharp end of the word bursting from his mouth in a shower of sparkling spit.

No one in town swore. I adored him immediately.

Neither of us was much hurt. He was completely unapologetic about his language,

Initiatory

either unaware of uncaring that he had used such a terrible word. I was glad. Everything would have been ruined if he had repented.

Let me describe him for you if I can. The memories of my childhood are mostly dark and rusted, and even Adam slips away from me now and then, if I'm not careful. But the way he looked is important to the story.

He was only a little taller than me, and just as thin. His hair was dark rich brown like damp earth and very straight, and I noticed right away that it was longer than other boys' hair. That's not to say it was actually long, of course. Male Mormons are well-groomed. (A sign at the college's dance hall: *Thank you for observing the grooming and hygiene standards.*) He wore things Mormon boys never wear: a tired old black t-shirt, faded denim shorts with rat-cuffed hems, a plaid shirt unbuttoned. This last was lying on the sidewalk. He picked it up, shook it out, and tied it around his waist while I righted my bike. He wore glasses with crackled blue-black rims. The lenses were thick and magnified his eyes, so that they stood out with a compelling intensity, each individual dark lash larger and thicker than it should have been. The irises were a darker blue than was usual, and the whites of his eyes were not white, but diffuse pink, redder around the edges, as if he had recently woken from a bad sleep. The intense color of his eyes and their prominence behind his glasses made him seem all eyes, so that everything in my field of vision, everything within range of all my stirred senses, was cokebottle lens and the downward mope of Adam's gaze.

His family attended a different church ward from mine, and so he was a virtual stranger to me, although we went to the same school. When he said, "I skipped school today. Let's go up onto the Bench," my heart burst and reformed itself in one quick beat. I liked the sound our bicycle wheels made, rolling together. I liked the look of our two pairs of shoes stepping in unison over the cracks in the sidewalk.

The Bench is the hill, a long, high promontory that slouches above the town, wandering up from the south. It slopes easily into the white and buff homes at the northeast edge of Rexburg, its gentle grade holding the temple and college up like pennants in the sun. It is a place for dry farming, home to the most famous of Idaho's famous potatoes. When the spring rains come the Bench flashes briefly into glorious, lime-green life, then settles back to its dry-smelling, dun-smelling slumber in mid-May, until the autumn snows set in.

Aside from the potato farmers, you will find no one on the top of the Bench but the wealthiest families, and at the start of the

Initiatory

summer when Adam and I were fourteen the ranks of wealthy families were growing. Construction sites pocked the spaces between clean lawns with their crab apple trees in glossy foliage. Valley-view lots were subdivided and allowed to tangle with weeds, dreaming of the backhoes that would soon dig the foundations that would hold the future rumpus rooms of return missionaries, who would come back to town to marry the girls who had waited for them. Business as usual, generation after generation.

Adam and I climbed steadily up the Bench, pushing our bikes. When the road leveled out at the long plane of acreage that would one day house the new temple, we got back on our bikes and coasted slowly, gear chains ratcheting, skinned knuckles grasping handlebars, wobbling. Startled grasshoppers clicked and glided along the road's shoulder. We rode all the way out to the blue and white water tower that reminded us in bent block script, REXBURG, an admonition, holy scripture engraved on plates.

In the grass behind the reservoir's cool cement wall, under the dark shadow of that same water tower, Adam and I sat on the ground, ate granola bars and half a cheese sandwich from his backpack, and nervously I held his warm hand. I rested my head on his shoulder. We talked of incidental things: town gossip, music, the end of the world. I sighed over and over because I felt good – better and more alive than I had ever felt before. And as the sun dipped and darkened and the shadow of the tower passed off our faces to stretch out across the potato fields into forever, I lifted his glasses off his face, looked into his sleepy dark blue eyes with all the fragile sincerity of a teen-age girl, and I kissed him.

Do not do anything to arouse those powerful emotions that must be expressed only in marriage. Do not participate in passionate kissing, lie atop another person, or touch the private, sacred parts of another person's body. Do not allow anyone to do these things to you.

Do not arouse those feelings in your own body.

Oh, Adam, your hand was so kind and eager, and your tongue in my mouth....

The prophet Alma taught that sexual sins are more serious than any other sins except murder or denying the Holy Ghost.

Why?

I loved you, Adam, and God made you. Or so I thought on that day, under the shade and spell of the water tower. I believed then that He made us both, as He made the grasshoppers and the Bench, as He made the colors of spring that grade into summer dull, that stifle under the thick snows of winter, temple-white.

Initiatory

3.

Did I feel guilt? Oh, yes.

When I was alone I would frantically pray, beg God to forgive me, cry great hot rivers of tears until the salt burned my cheeks. I swore never to do it again. I abased myself in my room with the door shut, face-down and trembling on my bubblegum-pink rug, but soon enough the tickling of the rug's fibers would begin to feel like Adam's fingers on my skin, and my shaking would turn to shudders, and a dark thick cloud of desire would eclipse my guilt entirely. The still, small, nagging voice in my head shut off like a light switch. Despair vanished, replaced by a bright pain of anticipation as I planned our next tryst. Sometimes I forced myself to recall the words I had learned in Sunday school, a half-hearted attempt to chastise myself into chastity: *Let virtue garnish thy thoughts unceasingly; then shall thy confidence wax strong in the presence of God; and the doctrine of the priesthood shall distil upon thy soul as the dews from heaven*. But that was no good at all. *The dews from heaven* made me think of wetness and the taste of salt, and the whole attempt at goodness would fall apart, and I'd get on my eager trembling bicycle and ride past Adam's house just to see if he was home.

Dating before the age of sixteen was

unthinkable in Rexburg – unthinkable in any Mormon community anywhere. Yet there we were, fourteen and depraved and absolutely in love. If Adam and I had been better children we would have heeded our lessons and removed ourselves from temptation. But there was the same slow current in both of us, the same slit eye. We were both inclined to question, both inclined to doubt.

After a few weeks of guilty prayer I no longer felt the need to beg God's mercy. My body had won this battle, and gladly I allowed it its victory. By July I saw the curved shadow of a monumental question mark fall across my town. By August I knew that the only truth in the world was Adam, and the feel of the hot summer against my back, and the whisper of insects in the long grass mingling with the whisper of our shared breath.

We didn't always do those things, of course. We had a proper courtship. We would buy Slush Puppies and sit on the hot curb outside the Circle K, discussing world events with an ill-informed fervor. With deprecating grunts and eye-rolls we would deny the accusations of our friends that we were "boyfriend-girlfriend." And best of all, most romantic of all, were our walks. As we wandered construction lots and potato fields that smelled of ladybugs and crushed leaves we would talk about anything – about all things – but mostly about religion.

Initiatory

It started innocently enough. One of us asked a question that skirted dangerously close to doubt, just for the thrill of it, just to see what the other said, a game of spiritual chicken. Who would be the first to admit the unspeakable?

"Do you think Joseph Smith was really a prophet?" I would ask, and Adam would reply, turning over rocks with the toe of his shoe, not making eye contact, "Yeah. Well, I mean, he could have been, right? It's possible." "But you don't think he really was." "I'm not sure. Do you?"

Or Adam would ask me whether I believed blessings were really from God, or were the men who gave them just saying what they hoped was true and right?

Was free will a plausible gift from an omniscient God?

Would the world really end in January?

Was it really so bad for us to do what we did together?

Finally I asked him the only question that mattered, the one we had both been hinting at for weeks but didn't dare touch.

"Do you believe in God at all?"

Adam looked out across the valley to where mountains folded into mountains into distant haze, where the river cut like a glyph into the ancient earth. He never did answer that question. But by then, I knew him well enough that he didn't need to.

Initiatory

4.

The day after I asked him whether he believed, Adam took me out to the acreage behind the water tower. We pushed out beyond a well-spaced line of poplars into a field gone to weed. It was green and lush, an ankle-high jungle of curling hot leaves and drying seed heads, alfalfa and tiny wild peas and stray viney potatoes.

At the edge of the field the land dropped away some ten or twelve feet, a sharp bank of exposed ocher-colored hard-packed earth spilling over with some scrubby plant heavy with tiny purple flowers. Below the bank lay a dusty pad of cracked cement, its edges and center eroding, yielding up handfuls of round loose stones from its crumbling matrix. It may have been the rotting foundation of a root cellar or a storage shed. Adam had found somewhere a box of old dishes, china and crystal, chipped, none of them matching. He had placed the box here already, right on the edge of the embankment. It waited for us in the sun. A spider had crawled inside. It scurried out of the way when Adam reached in, removed a teacup, and lobbed it into the air. The teacup hung a moment, suspended, glinting in the sun, rotating serenely at the apex of its arc. It threw a spark back into my eye from its gold rim. Then with a rush gravity caught it, and the cup hit the cement pad with a bright cardiac crash, a sound more exhilarating than a teacup had any right to make.

My heart pounded as loud as train wheels. There was a farm building close by, houses across the road, out of sight but not far off. Somebody would hear us. We would be in trouble.

I picked up a plate and hurled it into the sky. It caught on the breeze, banking like a crop duster. When it smashed against the cement I laughed.

He grabbed another cup with a very sad dinged rim and a broken handle. It was painted with a country-cute motif of hearts and flowers in subdued pinks and dusty blues, but the paint had rubbed away in places.

"I hate this place," Adam said.

"I know."

"What do you think a big city's like?"

"How big? New York big?"

"Sure."

I bent over the box to find my next projectile. Adam wore shorts; the darkness of the hairs on his shins struck me as very mature. I wanted to touch his perfect, geometric knees. Instead

Initiatory

I grabbed a cereal bowl. "I don't know. I guess it would be real busy and crowded. But I think I'd like it."

"Better than Rexburg," he said. There was something uncertain in his voice, something fearful.

"Better than Rexburg."

We threw our dishes together. The bowl and the cup struck almost at the same time. When the crash sounded, I recalled in vivid colors the look and sound of Adam cursing, picking himself and his bike up from the sidewalk, a spray of spit falling from his lips. On the cement pad, shards spread outward in fantastic patterns of chaos. I knew at the moment of impact that Adam was like a sliver of glass under my skin, pushed in deep where it could never work its way out again.

5.

It would never do to allow anyone in Rexburg to catch wind of the fact that Adam and I were in love. Sixteen was the officially sanctioned age for romance; we were two years shy. In order to maintain the summertime freedom that facilitated our secret passion, we had to keep up an appearance of trustworthy innocence. My personal goal was an air of wide-eyed, dimpled naivete, haloed in ringlets, and I chased that image with the focus of a serious athlete.

With sly calculation I allowed myself to be seen several times a week on the front porch, poring over the Scriptures, apparently just for the fun of it. I would dress in modest capri pants, in the sweetest pastel colors, sleeved cotton tops, not too tight, hair in good-girl pigtails, and I wore a furrow of concentration between my brows which I practiced daily in the mirror. I also practiced the distracted half-wave and half-smile with which I returned neighbors' greetings before pushing my nose back into my reading. If one can call it reading. My eyes moved over chapter and verse and vaguely some disembodied voice narrated unheard words inside my skull, while my eyes saw only the hairs on Adam's shins, or the creases in the skin over his clean angular elegant knuckles. And several times a week I

Initiatory

followed the neighborhood boys to the park to join in ball games or tree-climbing or joketelling, or any of the other simple things adolescent Mormon boys do in the summer under indifferent skies. I really had no interest in any of the neighborhood boys, or in their ball games. I participated because it was my camouflage. The more I rough-housed, the more the town would see what I wanted it to see: a tomboy who made a habit of running wild with boys, that was all, her chaste braids flying in the wind. Hardly unusual to see her roaming through the sunglowing weeds in a vacant lot with that Adam boy, the lenses of his glasses flashing white in a hot sun.

In the evenings just before dinnertime, body still reverberating with the echo of an Adam afternoon, I would sprawl on the grass of Porter Park with my girl friends. We nibbled candy bars or played M-A-S-H in our lined notebooks or made paper fortune-tellers, and talked about boys in hushed tones. I whispered along with them as if I knew nothing, as if I was the pure and good girl my modest clothing and soft smile suggested. I feigned shy interest in other boys our age and avoided all talk of that Adam kid. Katherine, Russi, and Danae tossed their hair in the sun and planned their futures: which boys they would marry, what they would name their children – and I went along, nodding and grinning, drawing on eyespots to conceal myself in the tallgrass tangle of their righteousness.

It was on one of these girls-only evenings in the park that I made a near-fatal mistake. The shock of my blunder firmed my resolve to keep my head down and blend into Rexburg's background at all costs. This is how it happened, as near as I can remember:

The four of us sat cross-legged beneath the birches. Above, the sky and the leaves conspired together. Katherine was all doe eyes and long white-blond silk hair; she picked blades of grass and twirled them between her fingers until they wilted and crushed and gave up their sweet summer smell. Her voice was as modest and subdued as leaves moving.

"Do you remember Sharlet? She was that sophomore who always wore hats and her family moved away in February. It's because she got pregnant. She's going to have a baby any day now. She might have had it already."

"What?" Danae was doubtful. Her face was already blossoming with the pimples that would permanently scar her cheeks later in life.

"It's true. They moved to Pocatello. Her whole family left because they were so ashamed. My mom told me. She heard it in Relief Society."

Silence. We digested the rumor. I flopped backward into the grass to disguise the special

Initiatory

thrill of terror I felt in my guts, the one I hoped did not show on my face.

"Well, I don't blame them," Katherine went on, "for being ashamed. Everybody would die of shame if I did something so bad. My family would probably drag me off to Timbuktu and I would just *die*."

"I'd never do that," Russi said. We didn't ask her what she meant. We all knew. I knew. "It's disgusting!"

The other girls giggled. I stayed flat in the grass and said not a word.

"Well." Katherine resumed shepherding our conversation with her usual gentle, melodic control. "I'm really sorry for her family. I mean, imagine feeling like you had to leave over something your daughter did."

"Pocatello." Danae stuck out her tongue.

"That's what happens when you go against Heavenly Father," Katherine said sagely. The girls nodded. Then – and I am still not sure why – I sat up.

"Who knows," I said, wondering what on earth I was thinking. "Who knows if it's really so bad."

They all stared at me.

"I mean, maybe Sharlet was in love. Don't

you think it's sad that she had to move away from the guy she loves?" Katherine: "I can't believe you'd say that. If she loved him she should have saved it for their wedding night."

"Well, what if God's not real? Then what's she saving it for?" Russi gasped and covered her mouth with her hands.

"Just think about it. What if?"

Katherine adopted an expression of pained disgust, deep disappointment. She was the charismatic one of our bunch, the popular girl, and when she turned that look on me I felt sick – literally sick, on the verge of throwing up right into the grass where we sat. In a rush my mind caught up with my mouth and I asked myself what I'd thought would happen, why would ever say such a thing to anybody who was not Adam. What were you thinking, what were you thinking?

In Katherine's wilted frown I felt the whole crushing weight of the town, the only world I knew, and the vastness, the finality of rejection from that small but very real universe. Perhaps I couldn't help my doubts but I could keep them to myself, and in doing so I could avoid ever seeing that look again on Katherine's face, or on anybody else's.

I made myself laugh. "I was kidding, you guys. Come on. I was just joking."

Initiatory

"That's not funny. You shouldn't joke that way."

"Lighten up. It was just a joke."

Katherine turned away from me. "I still don't think it's funny."

"I'm sorry."

*

I'm sorry. I'm sorry I wasn't like you, Katherine. I'm sorry the neat, defined life you loved so well never made me happy.

Truly, I am sorry. How much pain I could have avoided if I'd been like you, complacent and accepting and contented and good.

*

In the grass that evening under the birches, with my friends shrinking away from me, giggling with discomfort at my dangerous sense of humor, I realized that I could only be free with Adam. He alone understood me; he alone was like me. When we turned eighteen we would marry and move away, to some city,

New York big. We'd find a place where we could ask all the questions we wanted. Nothing would constrain us. Nothing would quiet us. We had four more years in this town, and then together we would cut ourselves free.

I lay back again on the lawn, let Katherine carry the conversation to safer ground, felt the flush slowly leave my face. I watched the leaves smile in the wind, and I thought of Adam looking out over the valley...*Do you believe in God at all?*...and the mountains folded into mountains, and the leaves into leaves, and the wind moved it all with a voice that was quiet and subdued, but never stopped speaking.

Initiatory

6.

Wind. Early August. Dust devils in the fields along the highway. After the requisite ball game I returned home for lunch, changed my clothes, and, shivering, remounted my bicycle. We were to meet on the Bench, at the remotest construction lot. The lot had seen no activity in a long time; Adam suspected it would remain abandoned until fall. My legs had grown stronger that summer from all my breathless biking. I no longer needed to push my bike up the hill. I rode so fast, in fact, that I arrived at our appointed meeting place a half-hour early, and expected to wait alone for Adam to arrive. But his bike was there already, slanting in the weeds against the pale green metal box of a ticking transformer.

I found him sitting inside the half-built house, sheltered from the neighborhood's eyes by a wall of flat, warm, naked wood. His back was to me, resting against one in a rank of two-by-fours that would eventually become a bedroom wall. He heard my feet on the bare, stony earth but did not look around. He just stared out at the valley stretched and drying in the sun.

"Hey," he said.

"Hey."

Baptism for the Dead

Silence. Nothing.

I came to sit beside him, hugged my knees to my chest. With my temple resting on my knee I watched his sad, solemn face. There were motes of dust caught up against his glasses, and the motes reflected the afternoon glow. Those eyes I loved so well, obscured by a haze.

"What's wrong?"

He was tense and quiet. I thought maybe he would break up with me. I thought maybe guilt had overwhelmed him at last, or he had heard the rumors about the pregnant girl whose family moved to Pocatello.

Then he turned to look at me, and the sun flashed on the particles of dust over his lenses. I blinked. The haze was gone. He watched me with those fantastically blue eyes. I saw that it was something worse than guilt. He did not speak for a long time, and my guts were all lit fuse, waiting for his revelation. When his voice came at last, tears came, too, sudden, tinged yellow in the afternoon light.

His parents were divorcing. He was moving with his mother to Seattle. He would be gone in two weeks. Gone.

I put my arms around his shoulders, but my hands were awkward and stiff. I kissed his hair. I love you, I said, and he said nothing.

Initiatory

In the desperation of that bleak afternoon, I gave everything I had to Adam's keeping. Soon enough we would be separated forever and only a few shards of this summer would remain buried in our skin. Dust devils in the valley stretched up and into the sky, conduits between heaven and earth that faltered and faded. We pressed ourselves into each other's flesh, scorcd the clay of ourselves with one another's nails. In the striped shadow and light of the unbuilt home I distilled Adam upon my soul, and he has remained there all these years, through everything, dew-beaded, salt and summer.

7.

In spite of my best efforts, still I feel I have failed to show you what Rexburg is. Everything is meaningless outside the context of the setting. You must understand the place to understand the story.

Listen:

Monday evenings the park is deserted. Every family is at home, gathered around a game board. Dad is the banker. He keeps the pink and yellow undersize dollar notes in neat little stacks. His mind is on the computer where he has hidden all his pictures of barely-eighteen girls in a folder labeled "Presentation for Client Meeting." The girls are tanned, their little breasts sharply pointed, their eyes dull, their mouths half-open in expressions of unquenchable lust or unfathomable disappointment.

Mom plays the iron piece. Her hair lost all its luster years ago; it's soft and rounded; she will put it up in curlers tonight, like every night, and recall when she was first married, how it thrilled her to brush her hair in front of her new husband, how he would watch her do it, come stand at her side and touch her shoulder and lead her to their bed. And she would think, Foreordained. For all of eternity I waited for you. And now she cries at night from the pain

Initiatory

of guilt because she thinks about her friend's husband, the man with the big hands and the smile lines that curve across his cheeks, his bold laugh and his lively eyes.

Each of their children – the dog, the shoe, the race car – they build up their fortunes and collect their cards and think, When I grow up I will have a family just like this one. Just like my own.

Relief Society meeting. The newest married girl shows off her two-carat diamond and pats her hair to be sure it looks just right. Everyone has brought a dish to share; the casseroles with lids are all labeled with strips of masking tape. They all look the same. The initiate samples every dish and compliments each woman on her cooking. She is thinking of the new husband waiting at home, his neat hands cradling a 7-Up in a sweating glass with ice. They were foreordained. This was all arranged ahead of time. Their children wait beyond the Veil to be called forth from her body, from her beautiful young body that was made by her Heavenly Father to be a vessel for life, a gift for her good, good husband.

His feet are up on the coffee table – she can see him, just so – his black trouser socks still on, just the way he looked in the pre-existence.

All of this planned, proscribed. Life after life carved in stone, life after life inscribed on leaves of gold. Golden plates hidden in the dark.

*

No, this isn't clear – not yet. Let me try again.

*

The red gem of the Gem State.

I can tell you that the streets are planted with shade trees, and every summer afternoon brings a gentle thunder shower.

I can tell you that the high school boys work in the potato fields all summer, moving pipe, saving up a tithe to pay their preselected wives when they return from their requisite routine missions.

I can say that the houses on the hill have open floor plans with plenty of natural light.

And all of this is true. This is Rexburg on the surface, and the surface is like the tense, bland skin on boiled milk.

When I was a little girl there was a pool in the

Initiatory

biggest park. A bright, decrepit carousel played calliope music and spun endlessly beside the pool, rattling, uneven, all summer long. When school was out I swam there almost every day with my brothers and sisters. A wooden hut in the park sold snow cones – my favorite flavor was tiger's blood, which was all the flavors mixed together with a distinct artificial note of coconut. My mouth stained red as I ate it, wandering the straight paths through the park, reading the boles of paper birches where teenagers had written their initials on the peeling bark in blue ballpoint pen. Each successive summer the old names were gone, flaked away, and new names appeared in their places, same identical hearts pierced by same straight arrows.

They filled in the pool the year I turned eight, moved the carousel across the grounds to house it in a forbidding dark wood fortress that choked the music in. Where there was pale turquoise water and horseplay, now there is a flat uniformity of grass, and they tore the snow cone hut down.

The trees peel off their unmarked bark. Every other week the grass is mowed and stray birch leaves are raked up, and the park is all green quiet, except for the breeze that leads in the brief routine storm.

Go out from the edge of town, past the

shirtless boys laboring in the fields, earning money for the wives they are yet to meet.

Go beyond the cemetery, beyond the lush line of the creek dark with cottonwoods.

Go to where the soil is still fertile but too rocky to tame, where the ground splits into fissures, heaves, craters.

These are the lava fields. Shining college and pure white temple spire and Relief Society and Family Home Evening, fore-ordainment in the pre-existence: all of it is built on the dome of a shield volcano.

The planet is asleep. But one day it will wake to the shout of a golden trumpet, and when it stirs, this town will be a vault of fire. American Pompeii: women frozen, smiling their identical smiles at identical electric ranges; dogs curled back in resigned arcs; men with their socks petrified to their feet.

The children, who will be the first to know that ruin has come, will leave their homes and run for the potato fields, and when the blast of heat reaches them they will be mannequins of ash, ashblonde hair and great leaping strides, arrested in their individual patterns of chaos, a V of birds shot down in flight.

Initiatory

8.

I was almost twenty-three when I met James, and that is why I married him. That, and he was good at making me laugh, and he loved books as much as I did. But mostly it was because I was getting old.

My sisters had begun to worry. My mother was pressuring me. My friends had all long since claimed their returned missionaries and hung the same glossy portraits on their walls: groom dipping bride on green-gold sward, temple of opal and crystal rising in the near distance, bride in modestsleeved gown with bouquet of roses, red and white, or of lilies, pink and white, or of callas, bloodpurple and white. Sixteen by twenty, matted and framed. My walls were bare. And I was almost twenty-three.

I met James at the singles' ward the one and only time either of us attended. We both figured that fact alone was some kind of message from God. I had gone only because it was expected at my age, unattached as I was, and sat through the sacrament meeting with an increasing sense of futility punctuated by the rhythmic clear plastic clatter of empty thimble cups of water tossed back into the sacrament trays. Drained little cups rattling.

Baptism for the Dead

I noticed James right away because his hands were so fantastically graceful, grasping the handle of the silver tray so smoothly, swinging it to the side, holding it for the next man in the pew to take and sip his consecrated teaspoonful of salvation. His hands made me smile. Physically he looked like all the other men in town: tallish, thinnish, short-haired, neatly dressed. But his hands were more descriptive, more refined. They moved like a music conductor's, measure and beat and sway.

He was new, just moved from Provo to accept a position as professor of English at the college. He was thirty-one, never married. He had a quick and very charming smile, the kind the author of an old-fashioned book might call rakish. His face, though, wore too much tiredness and resolve around the eyes. And there was an otherness to him, a careful way of moving, a careful way of looking about him, a softness of voice that lacked the confidence my friends' husbands possessed by nature. I knew right away. I could tell, as everyone could, I suppose, but never mind. That didn't matter. What mattered was that James, like me, had a secret. What were the odds that two people would meet, so perfectly and miserably matched? That too must have been a sign from God, I though wryly, remembering my Adam, throttling my urge to crack open the walls of the singles' ward with laughter or with fists or

Initiatory

with sobs.

We dated for three months – movies, lunch dates, walks in the park – and when he asked me if I would marry him I didn't hesitate. We could keep our secrets together. Short of Adam, he was the best spouse I could possibly have hoped for.

For his part, James knew I was observant and honest. He had commented on how sharp I was on our first date. That's what he called it: *sharp*. I thought what he meant was *You're not like the rest of them*. Sharp, so he must have known that I knew, even though I never said a word, not even to him.

James was sharp, too. Far sharper than me, to tell the truth. I am sure he knew right from the start that I, too, was hiding something from the world. But we never spoke of our secrets; not once.

We did speak often of starting a family. He desperately wanted to be a father and fawned over babies and toddlers, tossing them up into the air until they squealed, running them around the church lawn on his tall shoulders. Kids adored him. Parents respected him, not only because he was a professor but because he was making all the right choices, living the right kind of life. But although they respected him, none of them quite trusted him enough to leave him alone with their children. That always angered me. James was no threat to anybody, least of all to children. I wanted to call them out, shame them publicly for their ignorant assumptions. But to take them to task would have meant admitting *what James was* out loud, and that would never do.

Poor, sweet, earnest James. He wanted children, but he lacked enthusiasm for the required mechanics. Even hand-holding or long embraces made him uncomfortable, so after the first six months of our marriage I let him off the hook entirely, stopped trying to coax intimacy from him. It was for his sake that I stopped acknowledging the void in my life where some sweet fire, or at least a handy matchbook, should have been. We got into bed together every night with our books and our amiable nonchalance, and after the reading lamps were shut off, after the peck on the cheek good-night, we resolutely turned our backs on one another to sleep on our separate sides, in our separate realms.

There was nothing I could do to change the situation, and anyway, despite my advanced age I was in no hurry to become a mother. Instead I took a part-time job at the campus cafe, an acceptable pastime for a woman who did not yet have a brood to tend. It was not that I needed the money. James's salary was generous and we shared all we had equally. The job was an occupation in the purest sense of the

Initiatory

word, a distraction, a misdirection. I watched my modest paychecks trickle into my separate bank account the way a bored kid might watch ants in an ant farm fill a chamber with waste or with larvae. *Well, would you look at that.*

I did want kids of my own some day; just not badly enough to press the issue. Our pretense was much harder on James than it was on me. On the rare occasions when I brought up the subject of children, I deferred without protest to his usual line: It will happen when Heavenly Father wants it to happen.

That would have been some miracle. Acres of burning bushes.

On our wedding night he made love to me with his eyes closed, not out of passion but out of a sort of strained concentration, like a man enduring a dental cleaning. Afterward he shut himself in the bathroom for a long time while I blinked in bed, rolling the edge of the sheet between my fingers and trying to puzzle out what had just happened to us. When he finally emerged, dressed in a business-like bathrobe, he was all kindness and smiles. We put in a movie and watched it sitting up, propped against our pillows. My head was on his shoulder. His hand was on the remote.

You do what's right in Rexburg. Even if it is against your nature. Even if *you* are not right, you still do the right thing. That is what God expects, and so that is what the town expects. They all expected me to be happy with James. They all believed God had brought us together, and after all, we were sealed now for eternity. No going back.

I may have had no reason to believe in God, but I had plenty of evidence that Rexburg was real.

James and I had only been married a couple of weeks. Most of my things were still in boxes, stacked around the house, waiting to be unpacked and incorporated into my husband's home. My wedding gown was still at the cleaner's. James had declared the garden officially mine, and I was on my knees in the grass pulling thready weeds from between clumps of flowers. It was that familiar kind of Idaho afternoon, with light that managed to be both warm and blue, and slanted at a sleepy, idle angle onto the earth. I was thinking of dinner, of baking a spectacular dish of homemade macaroni with ham – something to impress my new husband, to make him feel he had chosen wisely in his selection of an eternal partner. I had, electrically pulsing in my middle, that special thrill of excitement which only new brides can feel over the prospect of macaroni with ham.

From two doors down there rose a sudden shriek – not the cry of someone hurting, but

Initiatory

a scream of rage. I stood – the knees of my pants were soaked and stained with grass – and walked down the drive to the road, to see from a polite and unobtrusive distance what was going on.

Marsha, nineteen, freckled, cute, sat slumped behind the wheel of her lime green pickup truck in the drive of her parents' house. Her face was buckled in upon itself, flushed with the heat of desperation and shame. Her father and brother solemnly carried boxes and suitcases to the truck, set them inside the open bed with care. I wondered whether it was Marsha who had screamed, but soon her mother emerged from the garage's open moaning mouth with a look of such fury that even I drew back, and Marsha drew back, cowering, her posture, her whole demeanor a ruin of distress. The mother carried something in her hands, an unfolded bundle of clothes. A load from the dryer, I thought dumbly as I watched her throw the clothes through the open window onto Marsha's lap. Marsha moved timidly, gathering them to herself.

"You will *not* stay here," the mother shouted, her voice raw and terrible. "I don't care where you go." And she kicked the tire of the truck with such ferocity that I turned and ran down the walkway, back into my house.

I hid inside while my mind fell all over

itself, trying to process the scene. Marsha had married a nice boy who had just taken over his father's printing shop on Main Street. Six months ago, after the wedding, they had moved to a two-bedroom fixer-upper on the west side of town. What was she doing at her parents'? Hours later, after I had wrangled my frantically prepared macaroni into the oven, I called Katherine to learn the news.

"Didn't you hear?" Katherine's voice was low and sorry. "Marsha cheated on her husband. Can you imagine! They only just married. He's already filed for divorce. She was staying with her folks but I guess they didn't know the cause of it until now. I don't blame them for being so angry."

"Where will she go now? Does she have friends she can stay with?"

"I wouldn't concern yourself with an adulterer," Katherine advised. And that was that. If I wanted to keep up appearances I wouldn't concern myself. Nobody else would, either.

I burned the macaroni. James laughed it off and scraped away the burned part, and ate the rest like it was caviar. I could hardly manage two bites. The sound of the mother's scream filled my head, and when I thought back on what I had witnessed that afternoon I could swear the truck's tire had sparked when she kicked it, as though the very force of her rage

Initiatory

had been made manifest. I thought of Marsha weakly gathering her unfolded clothes in her lap, as if she might put her world back into some order by folding them. I wanted to tell her to come stay with James and me; we had plenty of spare bedrooms, unoccupied as they were by children. But by now Marsha was long gone, driving out into the sage flats on a quarter tank of gas. She had always been a smart girl. She had already realized, no doubt, that there was no place for her in Rexburg. Not anymore.

But there was still a place for me, and so I didn't concern myself, and kept to my garden and my cooking and my husband, and hoped, with the fervency of prayer, that no one saw below the surface.

9.

The whole town suspected James's secret, but the whole town knew as well that we were doing the right thing together. That made us both redeemed, and made the thing he hid irrelevant. There was a time when I felt good about our marriage. I was helping him live the right kind of life, according to all the definitions of *right* either one of us knew. So what, that I wanted to hold hands and kiss on the Bench like I'd done with Adam years ago? So what, that my own husband never touched me with any real affection? I told myself very firmly that I didn't mind. But still, no matter how I tried to stifle the memory, Adam was with me, his smile and his laugh, the haze on his glasses, his mouth, his neck, the weight of him.

A good woman would have set these memories aside in some box of scraps and mothballs and forged ahead, allowed herself to be husbanded. For a while I did. I was good. But by the time our second anniversary came and went, I wanted Adam more than ever before – that sun warmth, the dust devils, the breaking glass.

In Rexburg you must always look for signs, for earthquakes and lunar eclipses. When you find a sign, you don't ignore it.

Initiatory

10.

Thursday was girls' night out. My friends left their kids at home with their husbands and congregated in a round green vinyl booth at Sombrero's. Pre-dinner, we restricted ourselves to a few tortilla chips each: baby weight to lose, for those who'd had babies, which was everyone but me. Artificial mariachi music wafted from speakers concealed by plastic plants while we talked about husbands, church, children. Occasionally the conversation tiptoed around the edges of sex, dangerously dirty. We stirred our strawberry lemonades nervously, giggled like school girls, and then Katherine guided us back onto the path of righteousness. Some things never change. Katherine soberly reminded us of the women in town who struggled with migraines, difficult children, endometriosis, any number of other trials provided by God in His wisdom. The rest of us nodded and frowned and made appropriate sounds of sympathy or disapproval, as warranted.

Thursday nights. Pick one. Throw a dart at the calendar. Every Thursday night was just like all the others before. Some things never change, except for when they do.

One very special girls' night out remains in my mind as the day my world broke apart. The day of the Second Coming. It was a disarmingly Rexburgian Thursday, which only served to underscore the drama. The early summer storm had rolled into Sombrero's parking lot. The evening light was olive green. Big warm rain drops pinged on the windows in an uneven rhythm. Young mothers hustled children into tan and green minivans. Husbands held up magazines as makeshift umbrellas and rushed across the wide street to indistinct red-brick buildings. Routine. Artificial music, artificial talk, artificial thunder storm.

On that Thursday, as it happened, I was the topic of our concerned discussion. This is an uncomfortable place to be in. Now I would feel justified in telling my friends to mind their own damn business, but those were the Rexburg days, the camouflage days. In those days telling off one's friends *was not done*.

Katherine's face was a pretty mask of just-so worry. She leaned across the table to winnow out my feelings on the subject of my apparent barrenness. I tried to be what I knew I should be: dutiful wife hoping for family. Soon enough, though, just as the waiter came by with a round of refills, I grew annoyed with being put on the spot.

"Twenty-five isn't old," I said. Most of my friends had their first children within a year of marriage – mothers before the age of twenty-

Initiatory

one – and were on to second and third helpings. But still, twenty-five is not old. "James says it will happen when God wants it to." The girls made their hen-clucks of agreement.

Katherine said, "Well, sometimes even God needs a little push. Are you two – you know – *doing what you need to do?*"

"Of course." Of course not.

"Maybe you should look into artificial insemination. Not by some stranger. You can use

James's...stuff."

I was about to ask her what precisely she meant by *stuff*, and then enjoy the sight of her blushing and floundering, when suddenly (thankfully) Katherine veered away from the subject at such a sharp angle that we were all seasick in her wake. She leaned across the table to whisper, "Look at that guy." Her eyes flashed, pointing without pointing.

Once I realized with relief that I was no longer under her microscope, I turned to look in the direction of her glance, and captured him in the act of sitting, just alighting on the cool green vinyl, a bird, a ghost settling onto a wire. Time bent backward in that long instant, the long indrawn breath when he emerged out of a memory otherworld. Rapid-fire series of impressions, in the order I saw them, in the order I felt them: plaid shirt open, faded cotton underneath, warm young hands very big, ragged pulse under my cold skin. Fiddling with his silverware. Dark hair, not neat but not messy. Heat rising to my face. The same eyes. He wore different-shaped glasses, but with the same thick lenses, and the remembered planes of his face were altered slightly by a new short beard. But the same eyes. Exactly, precisely the same: that particular shade of dark blue, the shot of red at the rims visible across the restaurant aisle, the thickness of the lashes.

For one hysterical moment I thought that Adam had come back to town. I was ready to run to him, throw myself on him where he sat slumped over his table, pushing a butter knife back and forth with one long, elegant finger. Just in time I noticed the differences between Adam and this man. These hands were too large and the fingers too thin, this nose too beaky, too prominent. But this – this resurrection, this miracle, these eyes – this was a sign, the kind of real, palpable, unmistakable portent Rexburgers only dream of finding.

A waiter stopped at the doppelgangers table, took his order. When the stranger spoke, his mouth was too wide, the teeth too large, almost comically so.

But the eyes were Adam's.

Rain pinging on the window.

Initiatory

"Who is that?" Danae whispered.

Quiet settled around our table while we all processed the intrusion: *Stranger. Not-us.*

The waiter edged up to the man's table, gingerly set down a bottle of beer, and sped away again. The man, still hunched with his forearms folded on the tabletop, turned his head a fraction. He smiled after the waiter past his angular shoulder. The smile turned into a dry little laugh, a private joke. His hand went around the beer bottle, and with his heavy eyes fixed on, looking through the tabletop he used his butter knife to press a wedge of lime through the bottle's mouth. The beer responded with a brief, shy, passionate fizz. The knife rose to his long mouth; his tongue appeared to lick the flavor of lime away; the soles of my feet pulsed, and I tasted in my own mouth the acridity of citrus and cheap metal. When he lifted the bottle to his lips and drank, his eyes met mine. I did not look away.

The man grinned.

He is definitely not from Rexburg, said Katherine's voice from somewhere inside or outside of my head.

11.

I was alone in the parking lot. The sky was pinking and purpling in preparation for a spectacular sunset on the heels of the evening's thunder. I hovered around my car, watched the wide empty streets. The wide empty eye sockets of abandoned buildings watched the innocuous pink and purple of Rexburg. I had faked an emergency text from James and left early, depositing my share of the bill on the table in folded fives and singles. The paving in the lot was still darkly wet, diamond-studded with rain.

I did not get into my car and leave. Not just yet. I felt compelled by some primal force to watch that man leave the restaurant, to see how he moved and to check this observation against the memory of Adam in motion. Then I would make my escape.

But when he produced himself from Sombrero's interior (heavy door sliding off fingertips, right hand in pocket, precise controlled swing of hip and knee) he saw me right away, standing beside my sedan, staring at him, and he came over (smile that was close to a smirk, squinting eyes that held me stiffly in place.) He said, "Hi."

"You're not from Rexburg," I said after we

Initiatory

had exchanged the expected, the wary smile from me, guarded; the lax shrug from him.

"No. I'm just passing through." Something like that. "I'm on sabbatical. Decided to tour the western States for a bit."

"But Rexburg, of all places."

"The light is good here," he said, as if that explained everything. He pointed to the clouds nimbusing eastward in colors of panic or embarrassment.

Through polite if somewhat tense conversation, I learned that he was an illustrator. Books of all kinds – the covers of novels, kids' stories, medical texts, manuals. Space ships abducting attractive women. Friendly dogs. Dissections. Team lifts. Grueling work, he told me, not nearly as fun as I thought it was, but it paid the bills. He had meant to see the West for a long time, and had finally saved up enough money to do it, to take as long as he wanted and just explore and draw and paint, get his creativity back, get back his passion for art after the drain of illustrating for years on end. He was on his way to Yellowstone, but had stopped in Rexburg yesterday for gas. He found all the houses fascinating: stoically alike and insistently pleasant. Ticky-tacky, he called them. He had spent an entire day secretly painting Rexburg homes from the camouflage hide of his car, on a block of watercolor paper he kept in the glove box. Did I want to see the paintings?

I did not. He was a mobile peeping tom and I had no wish to encourage him.

And what did I do?

The absurdity of the question. What does any woman in this town do? "I'm a wife," I said. "A wife," he said, considering. "Well, shit." There was no shower of spittle from Adam's lips but the feel of the word in this man's mouth was the same.

"That's not entirely true. I mean, I have a job. I work at a cafe part-time. And...and I garden. And I like to read." These admissions made me feel tiny and defensive.

"You're interesting," he said. His voice was deep, slightly nasal, low enough that I had to lean toward him to catch each of his words. "You're friendlier than most wives in this town."

For a moment the sound of his voice was all I heard – the note of it, I mean, the timbre. The words made no sense, as if my mind could only sort and analyze one aspect of his speech at a time. The umber hue of it, the dark wet honey – the whole world turned that color. His voice overtook me. Tickytacky walls of houses going transparent, and inside every bedroom fantastic and compelling scenes of fornication, all of them deep earth brown, lime and blue

Initiatory

metal.

Then I breathed in, blinked, and the meaning of the words caught up to their sound.

"Have you tried flirting with many other wives in town?"

He laughed. His smile canted up higher on one side than on the other, self-deprecating, totally disarming. "Not many. Only the ones who don't mind my beer-drinking."

"What makes you think I approve of your beer-drinking?"

"You didn't pretend I wasn't doing it. All your friends tried really hard not to look at me."

All my friends would be coming out into the parking lot soon. I realized I needed to get away from this man, or there would be probing, prying questions. And though we had only shared a conversation, I did not want the obligation of recounting it next Thursday. I wanted to keep it for my own.

"I need to get going."

Wait. He put out one finger – his hands looked too immature, like a boy's beautiful hands – and touched my wrist. The gesture was so foreign in its intimacy that I stopped moving, stopped breathing.

All my senses concentrated on the warm slender point where his skin touched mine. "You have an interesting look, and an interesting personality. Can I draw you?"

"Draw me?"

"I used to do a lot of figure studies. They're important. Anatomy – it's important, even if you're doing cartoons. I haven't done any figure studies in a long time, and I'd like to try a few. I'm out of practice."

"Figure studies? Like – nude?"

"The nude form is easiest to draw, but if you're not comfortable with that...."

"I don't think it would be a good idea."

"What's your name?"

I told him my name before I realized I probably shouldn't.

"I can pay you for your time."

"I don't need money; my *husband* is a professor at the college and I don't need money." "Just consider it, okay?" A card was in his hand; his hand dropped toward my purse. The card slid down between pocketbook and paperback, vanished.

"I really have to go now."

"Good-bye!" He waved at me and grinned,

Initiatory

and laughed down at my bumper while I climbed inside my car, shivering, and watched him shrink in the rear view mirror. Over and over I said to myself, Oh my heck, what just happened. It would have been easy for one of my friends to laugh off this conversation as an encounter with an out-of-town loon, a great story to tell at the next girls' night out. *Can you believe it? This creep wanted me to take my clothes off for him. He really thought I'd do it!* But perhaps because of his swaggering confidence, or because of his Adam eyes, or the way his voice looked right through all my walls, I realized slowly that I hadn't told him no. Not exactly.

Around the block where he couldn't see, I pulled to the curb and found the card. I read it several times before the words made any sense. His phone number and the word ILLUSTRATOR, the acronyms of a few professional organizations, and a detailed line drawing of a bird. And his name, of course: Xavier Pratt.

Final confirmation. Not Adam. Not Adam at all. Something more potent than Adam, and more compelling, my X.

12.

I took an art appreciation class in college. We were required to study nudes. This is startling curriculum in a Mormon school, and only barely acceptable because nude paintings by the Masters fall under the auspices of Fine Art. Everyone was embarrassed. They all tried to hide their nerves behind a sudden bluster of bookishness, a mass show of studious sobriety that only strained the classroom's atmosphere all the more.

But I was not strained. I envied the figures we studied. Like me, they had certain things worth hiding. Unlike me, they had bared their skin, their throats, their hearts, everything. And the result was not terrible, but lovely. People with all their privacies frankly expressed, athletic men in postures of stooped gravitational waiting, ready to surge up and hurl a discus or a javelin; women lying prone with loose-sketched faces, dense black triangles confronting the viewer with a dark texture and a decisive, knowing stroke of the brush.

I remember staring at each work of art as rapturously as a nun at the Madonna. The professor smilingly commented on my enthusiasm for the visual arts. It was not enthusiasm so much as desperation. In the

Initiatory

boldness of the figures I might find some example of how to turn my own sensitive pale nakedness out toward the world. Like baring a breast, I might declare GOD IS NOT REAL, and once the world's initial shock had faded, I might be framed in gold and displayed, admired, declared brilliant and brave. But no matter how I studied them, the nudes never offered any real help with my dilemma.

My fellow students, for their part, did not appreciate art appreciation. I remember one painting we studied in particular: a light-skinned woman lying prone, face turned away, long blonde hair tangled, hands lightly resting against the shameless, unashamed form of her own body. She floated against a black void as if pleasantly paralyzed in a dream. The crux of her thighs showed its flagrant golden hair. The other girls viewing the painting thought she was disgusting and unkempt, too coarse and too sexual. They said so with a display of moral banner-waving meant to draw the men in our class into their righteous and modest orbits.

I did not comment.

When I went to bed every night for weeks afterward I put myself into the blonde woman's pose, closed my eyes, and set myself drifting on a black velvet sea. I imagined there were watchers, analyzers of my composition. I dreamed the watchers could see right through my watercolor skin, but though I was an opened book, they pretended they could not read.

Within that dream I also dreamed of red berries in frost, and the parting of hair, and solo landscapes where white houses in brown fields waited for snow.

The watchers observed silently. They wrote papers on my dreams and I graded the papers and gave them all failing grades. Nobody understood. So nobody passed.

These were the best dreams I ever had.

Initiatory

13.

Back home, I kicked off my shoes in the mud room and shut the door to the garage quietly. No sound of television or radio. Kitchen abandoned, lights off, sun streaming in sideways through the valley-view windows, attenuated, rust-brown dust devil stretching up from my heart to heaven, wavering, breaking like a thread and retreating back into my body. James was not there. A note on the kitchen counter:

Sweetie – I went to I.F. For golf with the guys. Back late Saturday. J.

Golf with the guys. It had ceased to upset me more than a year ago. For all his faults, in spite of the total lack of passion in our marriage, I loved James. He was dear to me. I wanted him to have whatever happiness he could wring from this life, even if it was not with me. After all, I could never give him what he needed, no matter how dutiful a wife I was. I could not change the fact that I am a woman.

I am still surprised, even now, how quickly I came to accept James's trips to Idaho Falls. The way I saw it, he may as well have been sneaking off to visit a health spa or a psychiatrist. This was his therapy, and I would certainly not begrudge him a little relief from Rexburg. He was gone nearly every Thursday, Friday, and Saturday, thanks to a forgiving class schedule at the college; but he was always home in time for church by Sunday afternoon.

I had no idea whether it was always the same man he saw, or a different one every time. It made no difference anymore. We had stopped trying for a family long ago, but I still drove all the way out to Jackson twice a year to be tested, just in case. By now, devoid of all danger as our marriage bed was, the testing was an empty gesture, but one I could never make in Rexburg. Patient privacy laws be damned: tongues there would wag. They always did. Neither James nor I could afford to chance the rumor mill. I developed the habit of putting my husband's therapeutic excursions to good use. There was always gardening to be done, or house work, or reading, my great pleasure. I read more books than I could count during the two years of our marriage. It was a peaceful time for me.

Now, though, as I stood alone in my silent kitchen holding Jamess note in my cold fingers, the rhythm of the strange man's walk pounded in my temples. My skin flushed hot and prickly – the rhythm of him.

Tongue on knife.

Swing of leg.

Initiatory

Hand drop.

Card drop.

Laugh.

Good-bye!

James was in I.F., with some man. James was always going off with some man, and I never complained. It was Thursday, girls' night out, therapy day. Why not? I had a vision of Katherine leaning across the kitchen counter toward me, her face masked in studious worry: *Are you doing what you need to do?*

Somewhere between the car and the mud room, I had transferred the business card to my jeans pocket. I pulled it out and stared at it. I watched his name for signs of movement. I turned the card upside-down. I flipped it back-to-front, then back to the front again. And my cell phone crept into my hand, opened itself with an efficient muted flip, and the numbers dialed themselves, I swear, using the little hard callus beside my thumbnail, my hand under a smoke-lime spell.

He answered the phone: "Yello." rough baritone, very vibrational.

"Is this Xavier?"

"Maybe. Is this the wife?"

"So, supposing I do want to model after all.

Baptism for the Dead

This was a simple inquiry, nothing else.

Information-gathering, decision to be made at a later date. How do we do it? I mean, what's it like, and where would we go, and how long?"

"My hotel room is probably the best bet. Since you've never done it before, you can do seated poses, or lying down, if you're comfortable with that. It's easier than standing still. Holding one position for five minutes is a lot harder than it sounds; sometimes it's better to lie down. We can go for as long as you want to go – just a few poses, or longer. If you're comfortable with it, I can do a whole painting. That would take around an hour."

"I guess it kinds of sounds like fun. I mean, why not, right?"

"It can be a lot of fun. I'll make it easy for you. And I really appreciate it. You're helping me out."

"No problem, Xavier. I'm looking forward to it. I think."

"Call me X. Nobody calls me Xavier, not even my mom."

In the nervous shower, I shaved the stubble from my armpits and legs. I watched my face in the foggy mirror for signs of disapproval. None came. The steam from the shower dissipated off the mirror's surface. I got dressed, and with

Initiatory

a scrap of paper carefully held between thumb and forefinger (hotel address scribbled in red ink) I drove downtown to the Best Western.

The building was an unfocused gray; trees with gray-green foliage and gray-green trunks ringed it. I avoided looking around to see who might be seeing me. I bypassed the check-in desk, took the stairs. There was a faint mildew smell in the stairwell with chemical flowery overtones. The carpet was patterned and thin and seemed to drag at my feet as I climbed.

When X opened his door a square of yellow light fell out of the room, lit up my shoes in the dark hotel hallway. The dark fringe of hair above his eyes and the dark beard over his chin made his face a yellow square, too, which his wide mouth dominated with its slanting smile.

"Hi," I said. "I've never done this before." I watched his mouth, couldn't look at those eyes.

As I had knocked on the door a memory had risen up, a wisp of smoke in a distant field. Adam had wanted to be an artist, thought it would be cool, sort of glamorous or sexy, though as far as I knew he had never so much as doodled a stick figure in all his life. I wondered, standing in the hallway, whether I might read X in reverse, find a path in him to trace backward eleven years to Adam on the Bench with the golden dusty wind blowing down in the valley, an anagram, a palindrome.

Baptism for the Dead

"Well." X opened the door wider. He wasn't wearing any shoes, and his feet, absurdly long and angular with delicate, almost pointed toes, stuck out beneath the cuffs of his jeans. Feet shuffled backward over the hard flat dark green carpet. "Come in."

There were two queen beds and two small russet armchairs flanking a round table, three lamps in the room, all of them lit and giving off an unnatural, grapefruit-yellow light. Spread over one of the beds were thick papers of various sizes, deckle-edged, all of them bearing the images X had collected on his vacation. I examined them: cropland furrowed by rows of reflected sky; basalt canyons; elk herds; against an ocher hill, the innocent white steeple of a tiny church; overlapping that paper slightly, another depicting in dull browns and greens the burned-out skeleton of a building under a rainy sky. I looked at each one in turn, while X stood with his back to me (his shoulders were broad, almost as broad as my husband's), flipping through a sketch pad.

I said, "These are amazing. You're really good."

"Thanks. Can I get you something to drink?"

"No, I'm fine. Thank you. How long have you been doing this?"

"Art? Oh, I don't know. My whole life, I

Initiatory

guess. I've always liked to draw, but I didn't start painting until college."

"You have a degree in art?"

"Nah. I started one. I went to Cornish – big private art school up in Seattle. But I ran out of money pretty quick, and couldn't find any more. I dropped out by the end of my first year. Turns out you don't need a degree to be an artist, just a good portfolio. I guess I dodged a big bullet. Private college is expensive, and art doesn't pay well."

"Seattle?" Madam I'm Adam.

"Lived there my whole life. It's a nice town, though the people can be a little chilly and it's cloudy all the time. You ever been there?"

With considerable embarrassment I admitted that the furthest from home I had ever been was to Salt Lake City. And to the Grand Canyon with my family once when I was a kid, an unpleasantly warm trip in a big rented van that smelled faintly of vomit. I guess I'm not much of a traveler.

"You've never wanted to get out of Rexburg any more than that? Just Salt Lake and the Grand Canyon?" He let the sketch pad fall onto one of the beds. It had fainted from shock.

"What's wrong with Rexburg?"

X laughed a little. "You're tense. Relax. I'm

a professional. I'm not going to get weird on you."

"I'm not tense."

"Look at yourself in the mirror."

There was, of course, a dim mirror dominating the wall beside the television, the same mirror that hangs in every hotel room in America. In it I stood, blurred and orange-hued, arms crossed rigidly under my breasts, shoulders hunched. I found it impossible to tell whether the shine in my eyes was guilt or fear.

"Okay. I might be a little nervous."

"It's cool. It's normal to be nervous the first time you model."

"Have you modeled before?"

"Sure. I did it a lot in college to get extra money. In a school full of artists, nobody sees you as a naked person – you're nothing but shapes and values then, just the rudiments of form. I was scared shitless the first time I did it, but after a few minutes it was no big deal. I modeled for whole classes. Now that's an experience, standing up on a wooden box with easels all around you. But it was only scary for a few minutes. You'll see."

"You said I could leave my clothes on if I wanted to."

Initiatory

He only hesitated for a second. "Oh, sure! Whatever you want to do. It's fine, really."

He convinced me to sit in one of the armchairs, and though I refused a drink again, he pulled a glass bottle of iced tea from the mini-fridge, turned it upside-down and slapped the bottom in one quick, automatic movement; the metal cap responded with a sharp pop. He opened the bottle and set it on the table beside me.

The iced tea was probably caffeinated. What the heck, I though. In for a penny, in for a pound. I drank half of it in a single draft.

X shuttled his paintings together into a more orderly stack. He began sliding them into the sleeves of a big black portfolio case. "I'll just be another minute." When he had cleared off both beds, he produced a long wooden box from the space between bed and wall, flipped it open on the nightstand, and sorted through its contents. He pulled five or six bright turquoise pencils from inside the box, slowly and deliberately, examining the white inscriptions on the sides, then bit into the end of each one to hold it in his teeth. I watched in wary fascination. His tongue was just visible as he fit and adjusted the pencils in his mouth.

A strange, bitter, sharp smell, tangy and dark-golden, drifted across the room from the box. It was at the same time both penetrating and unobtrusive, just like the sound of his voice – and like his voice, the odor overwhelmed my senses, demanded my full attention yet received from me only a muddled, sleepy kind of dream-awareness.

"What is that?"

"Huh?" X settled himself on the furthest bed, facing me, and crossed his legs beneath him. He propped his sketch pad on one knee.

"That smell."

The pencils bristled up in a half-smile. "Linseed oil," he said carefully through his full mouth.

"It smells good."

"It smells good," he agreed.

X told me to arrange myself in a position that felt comfortable. Difficult, since I was vibrating with anxiety and no position felt comfortable for more than a moment. The armchair was hard, not evenly padded, and my stomach was unpleasantly knotted. Yet somehow I managed to keep still long enough that X nodded. He set his wrist watch. Beep. My hands rested lightly in my lap. My fingers felt cold where they curled in my palms. This was not a very dynamic pose, I knew, but for now it was the best X would get.

With the sketch pad standing on one corner

Initiatory

against the angle of his knee, he squinted at me, held a pencil in front of his eye and braced a thumbnail against it. The pencil slanted and drifted in the warm space between us. He measured me, marked a map in the air of my lines and proportions. The sleepiness vanished from his eyes. They sharpened, intensified; then he laid the lead of his pencil to paper and with a rapid, fluttering hand began to draw. In that peaceful scrutiny, that honest quiet moment, I knew that even if I had become nothing to him but spheres and cylinders, even if I was a transparent blur of color reflected on the lenses of his glasses, just then I was more real to X than I had been to myself or to anyone else in all my twenty-five years. Even to Adam.

The smell of linseed oil had so permeated the hotel room and my head that I felt the tingle of it on my skin, on the chair, on the carpet. The scratching of X's pencil was the honeyglow smell of the oil. I watched his face as he watched my unmoving body. His eyebrows – I had never noticed them before, but now I realized how much I liked them – they were totally unique to him, truncated little halfcircles, half-moons turned up to rest on their flat edges, and sparse, with his golden skin showing through the soft, fine hairs that scattered like fine powder. They were the kind of brows a woman would pluck and line, if a woman owned them. On X they looked not quite masculine enough to fit the rest of his face. I stared at his eyebrows for a long time, the way they moved, the way they jumped when he bent over the pad to correct a mislaid line.

Then his mouth tightened, and the pencils clicked together. And I forgot the eyebrows and thought instead that if I kissed him his mouth might taste the way linseed oil smelled, golden and dream-blurred....

"Hold still," he reminded me gently. "Sorry." Must have moved something at the intrusion of my thoughts. Keep still, keep still. Better not to look at him at all.

I let my eyes go out of focus. The white rectangle of the sketch pad doubled and softened, became two indistinct shapes that drifted apart minutely and came to rest at a slight, furry distance. Two light-furred Xes held two vague but identical sets of pencils in their mouths. I thought very hard about my breathing, and kept my eyes off his mouth, and held still.

Finally his wrist watch beeped. Five minutes up.

"Okay," he said. "You can move."

I stood. I stretched my arms above my head. X took the pencils from his mouth. He squinted at his paper, tilted his head, rolled his lower lip into his mouth and grabbed the little patch

Initiatory

of hair below with his upper teeth, sucked on it. The gesture was unconscious, bird-like and quick. He was beaked like a bird, that sharp hooked nose so unlike Adam's. How could Adam's eyes be a part of this stranger's face? And if this was a sign, what was the sign for?

Another pose. This time I tried to get a little more creative. I propped my elbow on the table and rested my chin in my hand, crossed my legs, put the other hand on my knee.

"That's good," X said, hardly glancing from his sketch pad. His hand moved quickly.

After that, another pose: slouched back in the chair, hands behind my head. This one was harder to hold; my back had begun to ache less than halfway through, but I kept still. I grew more comfortable with X's scrutiny; it no longer felt, in fact, like scrutiny. Each time he drew me, he raised the pencil to take a new measure of my body. Each time, I was light and shadow anew, shapes and lines, and this was just fun, just a little bit of Thursday therapy, nothing more.

By the fourth pose we were talking easily and by the sixth we were joking. And soon enough the pauses between poses grew longer. We asked each other questions. We sounded the other's depths. He had a nice smile – a big, broad, toothy smile and big hands and those impossible blue eyes.

Baptism for the Dead

I watched his hand move dream-like over his work, and I wondered. What would it be like to take my clothes off in front of this man? Would it be different from the way I felt when I undressed with James? With Adam? Would I still be shapes and values to him, even unclothed? If I showed him even more of me, would he see even more? This internal monologue was all very rational; I proceeded at a carefully measured pace, I considered my next move with a quiet, tight-reined control.

He finished sketch number ten or eleven. He asked if I wanted to see them all. I flipped back through the pad to the first drawing: his lines carried a strong, confident precision. The shape of my face was fantastically correct, accurate enough to be a photograph but softened, graced somehow by the pencil's fast silver strokes. Even my tension was apparent in the first sketch – even that, so I knew at once that I hadn't been wrong. X had really seen me, right into me, the stiffness of my back, the knot of my hands. And in each sketch that followed, he had noted and understood and communicated the loosening of my muscles, the relaxation of my fear, the growing ease of my smile.

"Well, if you want to keep going you're welcome to stay. You're a natural at this. I could draw you for hours. It is getting late, though. If you need to go...."

Initiatory

"No, let's do some more."

He smiled. Grinned – the right word for that broadness and brightness. "All right. Want to try some reclining poses?"

"Yes," I said quickly.

He gestured: I should make myself comfortable on the bed this time. I blinked and stared at it; it seemed to be dwindling to some dark green point on a wavering horizon, receding away from dizzy me and my cold hands and this private hotel room. But it was not, in fact, moving, I told myself sensibly. It was still right there in the same plane of reality where X and I bobbed and drifted, its coverlet as smooth and plain as a board.

"You okay?"

Yes, of course, all right, let's do this. Let's do some more. Let's take the plunge. James is off having his fun, so why can't I, why shouldn't I? Pull your shirt off over your head, drop it, unzip your jeans and let them fall. Movement of my hands like an autonomic response, and then the air of the hotel room pressing very cool against my legs which were bare now and my arms which had no sleeves now but not anywhere else, oh God this is bad, this shouldn't be happening.

X's eyebrows jumped. "I've never seen anything like that before."

Baptism for the Dead

Of course I was not naked. Of course; that's why the air was only cool here and there but not where it mattered. I looked down at the crisp white fabric of my temple garments. Oh, I forgot all about you, I said silently to them, my thoughts embarrassed and thick and stupid.

And then, a sort of visual cymbal crash, the whole scene brightening as if under flood lights, and the nauseating feeling that you are looking in on a movie starring yourself, out-of-body but entirely in-body: me standing there in my garments, two perspectives (my own eyes and some floating awareness peeking over my shoulder, very disapproving), and wrenching shame, and horror, and sin.

Just for a flash. The ringing residue of the cymbal petering away into tin whining, into silence.

Proceed with rationality. Tight-reined. There was nothing wrong here. I was doing nothing wrong. The lone audience looking over my shoulder expressed its dismay (its voice sounded suspiciously like Katherine's), then horror when it realized I could shut it up so quickly. But just like that I sewed its mouth closed with neat little deliberate stitches.

If James can, why can't I? I asked it.

And it knew it had no sensible or fair answer.

Initiatory

The flood lights dimmed. Katherine went to bed. I was only in a hotel room, standing in my sacred temple garments in front of a strange man. No reason for alarm.

"Want to draw me with these on?"

X was uncomfortable but too polite to admit it. I winnowed it out of the rapid blinking of his eyes, the slightly drawn-back posture. He was not the only one who could see what was right there before him.

I dropped myself onto the bed, wild, smiling, a girl at a slumber party in her pajamas. The mattress rebounded and in the slow-motion bounce I watched confused X blur down and up, all those pencils still hanging out of his mouth.

"They're called temple garments," I told him, trying to be helpful.

"Isn't that something I'm not supposed to see? Aren't they sacred? Isn't God supposed to get angry if you let me see?"

I stopped bouncing. There was something safe in X. He had Adam's eyes and that was a sign. I examined this final moment of my existence in a lovely crystal world, a world whose prism cast rainbows over everything. So simple here, this place where we all wore the same things beneath our clothing, where we all thought the same, all lived the same life. The air smelled of linseed oil and X's skin. Outside, far in the distance, a train called, a powerful sound bent and distorted by the agony of so much empty space. Its wail shivered. Night insects fuzzed in the gray-green trees. The fan unit below the window rattled to life and one quick breath of the outside air brushed the hairs on my arms. It was heavy with the smell of fast-dying grass, fading in the wake of the hot day's passage. Then came the smell of the building's recirculated air, clean and cold. And the sound of X's startled breath and the humming of the mattress springs, still alive with my weight. I had never spoken these words aloud before, not even to Adam. X was the first to hear.

"I don't believe in God."

I pulled the top off first, then the bottoms. I laid them not unfondly on the chair. I removed my bra and my underwear, settled back against the pillows, and turned my face toward X, and smiled at the movement of his hand as he worked, and the movement of his mouth as he frowned.

When night deepened I dressed again, but I left my white garments where they lay.

X asked, "Don't you want these back?"

I answered, "When can I see you again?"

Initiatory

15.

Just before James and I married, as I was preparing to receive the temple endowment I had put off for too long, I made a very special list on a little scrap of paper which I kept in my wallet.

Whenever I found myself questioning, whenever I wondered whether I really could survive, I unfolded that scrap and read my list. I did this so many times that I soon had it memorized, and the scrap of paper became as worn as soft cloth along the folds. Here it is, in exact duplicate:

Concealment (arctic fox, polar bear)

Disruptive (zebras, leopard)

Disguise (stick bug)

Mimicry (viceroy butterfly)

It helped to know that I was not the only creature who relied on camouflage to survive.

16.

Here is one particular memory:

Scene: shoe-white new Rexburg temple. Morning. Women's changing room. There are a handful of other women here, hanging their dresses in lockers, setting their clean shoes neatly side by side below.

Anxious girls of nineteen bunch together like slender glancing does. They have pale faces and tense thinned lips and wide, eager, shining eyes. Like me, they are here to receive their first endowments. At twenty-three, I am the eldest of the first-timers. My age sets me a little apart from their group, so that I can watch them with the detachment of a field biologist.

They don their sacred garments, drape themselves in long white over-gowns. There is such tension to their young bodies, so much fervency and fear. And all of that lovely sweet girlish energy is swallowed up and tamped out by the thick polyester gowns which fall down over their ankles with the swinging finality of a drawn stage curtain. *Finis!*

Bang of locker door. Murmured apology for the abruptness of the noise. On the bench, two parallel hair pins with a third crossed

Initiatory

over them, a slanted H. My toes blue and cold against the tiles.

The rest of the women, the older ones, move with peaceful surety. They are here to stand in as proxies. Soon they will be waist-deep in the great central font, baptizing the dead. They wear the same soft, far-off, unfocused smiles that they wear for their husbands and children. A few glance now and then at the young girls in their restless knot, the little school of white fishes shivering, and their smiles sharpen and tighten in sympathy, just for a moment. Then back to patting their hair, and dwelling delicately inside the boundaries of their own private territories.

My long white gown feels artificial and slow. But it is exactly as white as the other girls', and when I walk past them toward my curtained cubicle to be washed an anointed and blessed, I blend flawlessly against their mirage.

Sharp sniff. Quiet nervous giggle.

Oh heck, somebody whispers, picks at a torn cuticle, sucks a drop of blood from her finger.

I pass the older women, the distantly smiling ones, the vessels for the dead, the dutiful happy body doubles. They got up early to curl their hair, even though all that hard work will soon be ruined by the water in the font. Bend them backward again and again, again and again, immerse them until all the lost souls are free, and their flesh is wrinkled and softened and running with sanctification.

Rattle of the white curtain being drawn back. Smell of textiles, hair spray, and faintly, an undertone, chlorine.

I wonder as I enter my washing cubicle (a cool hand dabs a droplet of clean water to my forehead) whether there is some other world, some other reality, where a kind, sharp-eyed, straightbacked woman stands as a proxy for me, and undergoes a secret rite that will free me from my snare. As I am anointed with a dab of oil at my hairline, I imagine her naked and yellow-haired, bent backward into a black ocean, and when she rises up again, streaming with dark cold water, her smile is as bright as a slashing knife.

*

Now, of course the goings-on inside the temple were sacred and therefore secret. I could only discuss them so far with my friends. And I had to take care in how I approached the subject.

I could no longer avoid the temple endowment. I had already put it off for years.

Initiatory

Further avoidance would have made me more conspicuous. I settled on approaching it like a scientist, a curious observer who was not truly participating but only gathering data. And once I'd completed the ceremony and received my sacred garments, my desire to compare my data was overwhelming. In order to get my friends to talk somewhat freely about the temple, I had to veil our conversations in glowing feminine zeal, just the right balance of enthusiasm and humility. I did this without difficulty. I was adept at preening my camouflaged feathers.

With my head to one side and a thoughtful half-smile I asked Katherine what she had felt during the ceremony.

I expected her to reply that of course she had felt the Holy Ghost fill her heart, or words to that effect. Expected words, the rote recitation. I was not expecting the reaction she gave. Katherine paused in the act of stirring her cake batter. Her eyes swelled with tears. "It was…it was amazing," she said. Her arms trembled. Her spatula rattled. "Oh, how can I even describe it? Like a fire inside me, like…" she trailed off, tears streaming, half embarrassed at her own rapture. She set down her bowl and walked to her kitchen window, folded her hands at her throat, and stood in the slant of natural light, smiling, eyes closed as if in prayer. Outside, children shouted in the street. Katherine sniffed. "I have never felt so alive before," she said. "I finally knew what being alive really means, for the first time."

Now this threw me. I had thought I had felt the Holy Ghost a time or two in my life, when I'd prayed for guidance on the big questions that plague a child. Should I tell on the boy who had stolen the notes to the history test? Was it moral to have two best friends at the same time? And even when I wasn't praying, the feel of the Lord's love and assurance would sometimes sneak up and overwhelm me, fill me with a shiver of awe when I contemplated creation, prophecy, eternity. But nothing in my admittedly limited religious experience had ever moved me as the temple endowment had evidently moved Katherine. I watched her tremble and shed tears of joy and watched the air go out of her forgotten cake batter, and I wondered just what was wrong with me, anyway – where this brokenness in me had come from.

I tried another approach to my research: Danae. We walked through the park and I told her how impressed I had been with the temple, how it was an amazing experience – and then I allowed my voice to trail off temptingly, and I prompted her with a goading, "But...."

She gazed at me with concern. "But what? I've always thought it's wonderful. I just love it every time I go."

Initiatory

"But nothing. It was nothing. Never mind."

I did do my best to kindle the same passion for the church which everybody around me seemed to possess by nature. I threw myself into the study of scripture, committing two hours a day to reading and contemplation, although this experiment lasted only a week. Each day I found myself staring at the illustrations in my Book of Mormon, ultimately contemplating nothing.

There was one illustration all Mormons know as surely as they know the faces of their mothers: Joseph Smith the boy cowering in the forest, crouched in the leaf litter, a hand raised to shield his eyes as, in a terrible halo of white fire, Jesus and the Father gesture toward him, as nonchalant as a pair of housewives selecting melons in a supermarket. I eyed this illustration for days, hoping it would fill me with a small measure of Katherine's passion. But the more I looked at it, the more the figured blurred. Eventually the sharpest and brightest things in the painting were the leaves, the woods themselves, the thickets where implied animals hid like the beasts in medieval tapestries, their necks curled backward at savage angles, brutal and waiting. I imagined that when young Joseph had stood and staggered back to town, smudged with the soot of revelation, the creatures of the forest emerged to slink down their hidden tracks and sniff the air, lithe bodies blending into shadow. The animals would taste the odor of a single man on the air, faint, ordinary, and already fading.

*

For months after I'd earned my temple garments they felt raw and unfriendly. My clothing moved now in strange ways, poked or pulled at armpit or hem by the fidgeting of the holy garb underneath. They made my body an inelegant blocky half-sculpted form, a stiff incomplete maquette. Ugly puckered seams turned the roundness of my breasts into slack hanging rumpled white, an old lady's chest. No definition at the waist, so all the soft curve I'd been so proud of was gone in a flash of ceremony, poof: Grandmama in her unmentionables. To shower, to swim, to remove them for any reason at all was a relief. But of course I never told anybody about that.

I knew none of the girls would admit to feeling relieved at being rid of her garments for a quick shower or some illicit sunbathing, even though they must feel pleasure in their own nakedness. They must. I assumed all the girls felt the same way I did, but of course I expected them to pretend these underthings were everything they had ever wanted. These

Initiatory

were our sacred garments, the markers of our Mormonhood. We would all just have to learn to live with them. *I* would just have to learn to live with them, because that's what good women did.

The week after my endowment ceremony, long before my body had grown used to the feel of the temple garments, I went shopping for shoes in Idaho Falls. I passed, by chance, the lingerie department of one of those big stores with the oatmeal tile floors and the sales girls in button-up shirts. Little bras and panties hung in matches sets, cute, two for twenty-four dollars, pink and teal, thongs and bikini cuts. And I thought, Well, what's the point now? What's the point of any of that cute stuff, ever again?

Then I remembered that I was about to marry a man who wouldn't much car whether I wore a pink thong or shapeless holy garments or a gunny sack, and I laughed out loud right there in the store until the sales girls stared at me and whispered. Leopard, I reminded myself. Viceroy.

Such funny things, those garments. Funny that X opted not to draw me wearing them. What a sketch that would have made, what a nature study. The field marks of the good wife: white throat, white belly, white on white with an oily crown. Oh, my X, what an opportunity you missed! And by the time our first evening together was over, all you had left was my molted coat, a specimen skin discarded on your hotel chair.

Creation

Creation

1.

if a strange man comes through your town and asks you to model for him...

if a strange man comes through your town and you see him drinking beer in a restaurant...

if a strange man comes through your town and his eyes are just like those unforgettable eyes, oh the warmth of summer at the top of the Bench where the wind moves the scent of growing things, where the wind moves the scent of potatoes and dust and alfalfa drying in the sun, where the wind moves your bodies in a shy rhythm where the wind smells as sweet and earthy as his skin

if you want to blend into rexburg (Concealment Disruptive Disguise Mimicry) you must be as simple and clean as a long white gown, as alike as bricks in a red wall, as straight and featureless as a steeple.

I saw a strange man drinking beer in a restaurant. He was as sweet and earthy as long grass drying in the sun.

I saw a strange man in a restaurant, and the wind moved over me, and I was as simple and clean as a blade of grass and as hungry as Adam in the Garden.

Baptism for the Dead

You want to blend into Rexburg, but you are as stark and unbroken as a steeple. You are only a brick in a broken red wall. You are only a blade of grass, and the wind will move you, and the wind will move you.

Creation

2.

The night of the modeling I couldn't sleep at all. The bed I shared with James Sunday through Wednesday felt emptier than usual. The sheets crawled over my bare skin. Eventually I kicked them off and lay naked and chilled in my bedroom while the moon swooned over the distant Snake River. I hadn't felt sheets or night air against my exposed body for more than two years. Was it the lack of temple garments or the tight, hopeful, hopeless knot in my stomach that strung me up in such a state of discomfort?

I moved all night in an unpleasant trance, not awake and not asleep, hemmed by the naked bed's edges, a gray restless territory with stern boundaries. Every hour or so a lone car approached up Poleline Road; its headlights crept through my blinds and pulled me fully into consciousness, and I would look down the length of me, foreign and vulnerable and zebrastriped with transient bars of shadow and light. Immediately I would lapse back into a blur of half-sleep where the shadows became dark pencils slashed across the mobile brightness of X's mouth. And the cars passed, and the illusions passed, and I stumbled through a blurred forest on weary feet, chasing the clarity of deep sleep, a stricken and ineffectual hunter.

Baptism for the Dead

I knew that I loved you, X, but I didn't yet realize I knew.

Sometime around three in the morning I woke and saw that I would not haze back into semisleep again. My heart was hammering with some inconvenient second wind. My eyes were like eyes at a bonfire, burning and purple-scarred by the memory of moving light. Not knowing where to go or what to do, only that I had to move, I dressed and pulled back my tangled hair, and got into my car.

I drove west without a plan. Houses dark, roads empty. Here and there a single lit window cast its orange glare over cottonwood leaves and I caught in passing the dark fast silhouettes of mothers tending sick children, men up too late, sleepless and vague with worry. Pumpkin-orange light, rapid silhouettes.

Once I reached the highway I drove with a hawkish alertness. My destination had decided itself. North Menan Butte is the dead volcano's proper name, but everybody in Rexburg calls it R Mountain, for the big ugly white letter branded onto its northeast side, facing the town. The R is a mark of ownership. We took possession of the place, claimed it for our own, and it is as obedient and good as any Mormon. Extinct volcanoes tend toward an appealing tractability.

Creation

James always liked to call it Our Mountain, and I would say, *Very punny* in a tone of mock annoyance. James and his word games. James the extinct volcano. James with an R over his heart.

The sun would not be up for another hour at least, but already the R on the butte's flank was fading into view, bird's-egg pale asserting itself against the plush black of foreground mountain and background mountain and valley and sky. I drove toward that weak beacon like a sailor toward a pole star.

The parking area near the trail head was empty, of course. No one goes hiking before dawn. The air was cold even through my layers. I pressed my hands under my armpits. There was enough starlight and enough of a retiring half-moon to find my way up the steep trail to the rim of the crater. The ground was hard and dark, and I was grandly alone, and out of breath. I hunched at the top, leaning on my knees, my cold hands braced. The heat of the climb slowly passed off me. I began to shiver. My body and my mind were both exhausted, but I have always found that I do my best thinking in such a state.

True stone-heavy weariness strips away all superficial concerns and only frank rationality is left.

Baptism for the Dead

Options are narrowed and sorted. Questions ask themselves.

Far below me, Henry's Fork turned the same matte deep violet as the sky. The pale pointillist reflections of stars fainted away. A growing shimmer of light spread down the twisted length of river, east to west, bluing and brightening. Irrigation canals revealed themselves among spectral wheat fields. Retention ponds gleamed like sunken gems against featureless, pale skin.

When I was lying on that hotel bed, bared clean, I was as deep as this valley, I was as complex as stone. When X's hand moved over the paper and revealed me, I was as singular as the river, as distinct as the clear cut of mountains against the warming sky, there on the eastern horizon, where I could see off into a distance grown rapturous with light.

Questions ask themselves, and answers form like land rising from the water. And oh, the sky at dawn is beautiful, beautiful.

3.

Dawn.

Sky wheat-gold, skin-gold.

A sunrise like the first sunrise, soundless and welling. The last star held, wavered, wilted. A dulled half-moon sank placidly behind the distant Bench.

The sun glowed like the smell of linseed oil. Its light fell on my hands, a square of light falling onto a dark floor; color of warmth, color of X's skin.

4.

It was early June, and the great flat expanse of the Snake River Basin lay like an olivine quilt, a thin assemblage of rectangular and round patches stitched by lines of dark cottonwood. From the top of Our Mountain I watched the Basin stretch away into an impossible distance, a dizzying flat of muted greens and emerging gold whose horizonward crawl felt as slow and inevitable, as certain as the Second Coming.

Above, the morning sky blued into eye-blue, overlaid with a delicate dawn-pink mackerel lace. The sky in its hugeness was overpowering. I felt compelled by its one great ever-open eye to crouch down on the trail, as if by making myself smaller I might escape the scrutiny of such an honest stare. In the sky far to the west, pale lines of cloud drifted together, lazily considering a convergence but in no hurry to get there; their movement was unfocused, of no pressing urgency (it's all inevitable, certain in the end.) Sky and earth never met at the horizon, but confused themselves in a brown-violet haze, a dwindling somewhere just beyond the irregular line of tiny distant mountain ranges.

The surface of the butte was minutely alive, moving constantly in a rising southwestern

Creation

breeze, a visual disruption like snow on a TV set. Low, long-stemmed plants shivered. The constant wind carried the scent of growing sage from deep and far into the valley, the bright warm tang of sun on dry yellow stone. The movement and scent of this place comforted me. The dawn air tasted of water in a glass.

My body trembled with a satisfying combination of cold, weariness, and revelation. Weeds with glaucous leaves shivered in sympathy. Everything was rooted in place. All these little stragglers holding fast, the thin evening primroses with uncertain buds, fiddleleaf and blazing star, every one of them dug down deep.

Send out your seeds by burr or by bird. Send out your runners just feet away. Generation after generation with roots wound up together in this hard yellow soil.

*

Birds woke downslope. The brush-covered flank of the mountain volleyed with song. I walked the trail along the rim of the crater, watching specks of birds in bounding flight over small fields. They scattered like poppy seeds spilled from a spoon. A falcon rose up from nowhere, rotated slowly on the high morning air, dropped to earth again to merge with the golden-brown plain.

Three mule deer moved far below me, drifting between stands of sagebrush, vanishing among the thickets, re-emerging as hesitant as ghosts. From the remoteness of the river, which was no more than a silk cord dropped along the length of the valley, a cow's bellow rose up broken and faint like a heartbeat.

The sound of earth and rock shards under my feet. The sound of cold wind. My nose ran; I wiped it on my sweatshirt's sleeve as I walked. Rapid diagonal dash: the motion blur of an unseen lizard. I looked in the direction of its flight. Nothing. Then, as I drew closer, it zinged away again, far off the trail and up among a stand of boulders. It had been nearly under my feet; I hadn't seen it at all. As long as it held still and pressed itself to the earth it was invisible. But when it moved, it cut across the bland landscape like lightning in a gold-dust dream, and though it was only a simple, small creature, the impossible speed of its movement made it seem as great and fearsome as a dragon.

5.

Weariness always makes my thinking easier, my thoughts more starkly defined. Why should that be?

When you appeared on the rim of the crater, X, pausing and gathering the morning in, all my questions were asked and answered. You do not ignore a sign.

The sun had finally begun to warm the dew from the air. The mountain was rich with the scent of the day's heat to come. I started toward you on the trail. You started toward me, your knees-out, goosey walk, your long arms swinging, a small muscle deep in the soft crease of your elbow twitching.

Of course you would come to the mountain this morning. Of course.

I was nauseous from hunger and lack of sleep. I was a dragon speeding among the pebbles. When I reached you, neither of us spoke, but I reached up to your mouth and kissed you.

Your kiss was wetter than I expected it to be, your mouth rougher. Your hands on my back were warm. When I raised my own hands and laid them against your body, the trace of your ribs beneath your shirt was like the bowing of a river.

Garden of Eden

Garden of Eden

1.

We had a couple of hours yet before the parking lot filled up and the butte's trails became lousy with teenagers. X and I walked out to a great rippled dome of black lava and sat close together, sharing a muffin and fruit from his backpack while the valley yawned. He had come to sketch the view, but his plans had changed.

A little food in my stomach did me good. The stark smooth slope of lava rapidly drew in the morning's warmth. Like a lizard on a rock, I thought, and stretched, and reveled in the tired humming of my body. I was ready for sleep. I could have slept right there on the exposed ground, with the world mumbling and minutely stirring far below, but every particle of me was hyper-aware of X's closeness and warmth, and my mouth was still electrically pulsing with the feel of his kiss.

A little tangerine-slice segment of my brain was aware that I should feel terribly guilty. The rest of my mind – a much bigger and louder and juicier portion – wondered at the fantastic paradox of physical exhaustion and hart-lurch that was turning my muscles and bones to honey.

Baptism for the Dead

X told me stories of his short time in college, and of the week of his road trip before he had arrived in Rexburg. I listened to the cello note of his voice in a sun-stupefied trance. His words ran together, a thick warm slow-moving river. There was nothing in the world to concern me but X and his currents.

When the sun grew so bright that we had to squint, I led him along the trail to the caves, shallow sharp cuts back into the basalt of R Mountain, still dew-cold and dark. We settled into one, shoulder against shoulder, thigh against thigh. It took my tired eyes a long time to adjust to the violet shadow of the cave; X obscured and twisted into thrilling shapes within the dim reach of my blinking, bleary vision. He was all kinds of possibilities. X the escaped convict. X the Soviet spy. X Pratt the expat. In the shelter of the caves he and I could have been anybody, any assortment of nobodies, without past or obligation. But soon enough my fogged vision cleared and there we were, just us, a cheating wife and an itinerant artist hunched in a cave looking down on Mormontown. There was something Cro Magnon about the whole business, rather depressing and doomed but earthy and sexy and wild, ancient and impermanent.

"So you're married," X said.

"Kind of."

Garden of Eden

"Kind of?" "I'm not sure you can really call it a marriage." Long, long pause. Distant sound of an engine. Distant sound of a barking dog.

X drew in a breath and I knew he was about to break the silence, but I needed to make it clear to him first, this whole fiasco, my life. My stomach was tender and tenuous around the hollow of my exhaustion. I dropped words I had sworn I'd never say like little uncertain gifts into X's hands.

"My husband is gay."

I didn't know what to expect. Two years never saying those words...there must have been some reason why I'd never said them, some Curse of the Cat People, some hex. But nothing. No lightning fell from the sky. There was no consequence. A dumb insect clicked and tumbled in the scrub outside the cave's mouth. A breeze stirred the sagebrush. Years of painful silence amounted to this: nothing. "Jesus," X said.

I stared at him stupidly.

His brow was furrowed. "Why did you marry him if he's gay?"

"Well, everybody's supposed to get married," I said, suspecting that what I said was idiotic beyond all measure.

"Why?"

The appropriate response would have been, Because that's what God wants us to do. But I had already outed myself as a nonbeliever. I had dropped the camouflage act back in his hotel room. I had no good answer, for him or for myself, and the sudden realization of that fact embarrassed me. I settled on, "That's what everybody expected us to do." Which was, of course, the truth.

"Everybody? Who? Your families? Your town?"

I nodded. I could not speak. The injustice of my situation had finally revealed itself in all its enormity. It was a great ugly monster of a reality. Why had it taken me so long to see this? But of course, twenty-five years of Rexburg could not be shaken loose as easy as that. There was marrow in the bone.

"You don't understand what it's like, living here. You don't just do your own thing."

"Why not? What's the worst that could happen to you if you did?"

"Anything. Everything." My whole family... everybody I've ever known... Total and absolute isolation. Allowed to live among them, but functionally banished, a social leper. Or worse. Driving off into the sage flats on a quarter tank of gas.

Garden of Eden

X, I couldn't make you see it. You didn't understand.

He did see that he had struck a well-worn nerve. "It's all right." Awkward in the closeness of the cave, he put his arm around me, very warm against the coolness of our refuge. "What's your husband's name?" he asked, a diversion.

But the thought of my husband was not a pleasant distraction. James may be well versed in adultery, but this was all very new to me, and I was not prepared for the sudden rasp of remorse. It came out of nowhere. I covered my face with my hands and said, "James," miserable.

There was a pause and a pyramid of rock chips outside the cave's mouth, reflecting the bright sun.

X, quietly: "I feel sorry for James. It's cruel, that everybody should make him be somebody he's not."

The simplicity of those words. X was right. For God's sake, I had never thought of it that way. James had always been doing the right thing, fighting against his nature as if it were an affliction. If he couldn't keep it entirely at bay I could not fault him for that. I couldn't keep my doubt at bay, either; the least I could do for brave James was honor his desire to blend in and give my tacit approval to his trips to Idaho Falls. It seems impossible, I know, that I had never realized until that moment how backward we all were. The suggestion that James was not afflicted but rather victimized was so novel it stunned me. I had lived my whole life in that town. There is marrow in the bone, and the bone does not break easily.

Garden of Eden

2.

X left his car right out in my driveway for the world to see. No one in Rexburg drove a hybrid; it was obvious as sin. I could have had him pull it into the garage but by the time we made it to my big house on the Bench I was far too tired to care about propriety.

Ground clouds had settled by midmorning, veiling and lowering the sky. We would have thunder in the afternoon for sure. I made some token gestures toward hospitality, pouring lemonade and getting out a box of ginger cookies, waving X toward the back porch that looked south and west to the side of the very mountain we had just climbed, blue and indistinct in the slow-gathering clouds. The R was hardly visible. I collapsed into a deck chair, my whole body vibrating with the need for sleep.

X asked me questions.

Had I always known about James? I had.

Where was he now? Off with his...his boyfriend, I guessed (had never said that word, either.

Strange thing to say so matter-of-fact, my husband and his boyfriend.) Every weekend, or just about. As far as I knew he was always with the same man and I had gotten all the tests and was clean, thank God.

"Thank God." We chuckled at that.

"He must love this man over in Idaho Falls." I guessed so. I was glad James was in love.

"You're not jealous?" "No." Simply.

"Why not?"

"I want him to be happy. I know it seems strange, X, but he is my husband and I do love him. He deserves happiness. This life we have together...this isn't enough for him."

"I guess not."

"How could it be?"

A neighbor's cat broke from a line of shrubs, ran rabbit-hopping down the slope of the back yard. All the dandelions had gone to seed.

"Well, what about you?" X said.

"Me?"

"What are you getting out of your marriage? Happiness?" X had one leg stretched along the length of a slatted wooden footrest. The hair along his shin was dark just like Adam's. "Have you ever been in love?" he asked me.

I turned my face toward him, nodded,

rested my cheek against the warm wood of the chair. "I've had it," I said. "I've had enough of this place."

There were fires in the fields. Across the dim ocher expanse of the valley, wan columns of smoke rose and wavered, broke apart on the wind. I imagined that to the farmers tending those fires, the smoke was strong and thick, the fire hot and close, fearful in the way it consumed the remnants of their fields. The smoke stung their eyes until they poured with tears; above them the wind scattered their offerings into nothing. They threw more and more and more into the flames, but always the valley wind smeared their altars with an unseeable hand. When the last of the withered stalks went into the flames they would say with uncertainty, In the name of Jesus Christ, Amen.

From my view deck on the Bench, with X backslouched into his chair only a foot from my hand, all the threads of smoke looked weak, and pale, and the same. In the gray-green margin where the wind took them they blended into a seamless haze, one bank of fog below the fogged and motionless sky, one mournful spirit that crouched, hesitating, over the still fields. From where I sat, all fires were the same fire, pleading the same mute prayer. Al the votaries recited their testimonies in identical, passionless words, learned by rote, but the right words, by God, In The Name Of Jesus Christ Amen. Do what you are told and no more, and no less; the hand of God will blur you into one pleasing gray formless haze. Like a child finger-painting.

Birds tumbled through the haze, through the smoke bank soft as prayer. A fly walked on the rim of my glass. Its tubular mouth touched, tapped; then it lifted into the air. X's hand drooped of the end of his armrest, long fingers slightly curled.

Inside the house, my phone buzzed to alert me that Katherine had left a message inquiring about a strange car in my driveway. I would never return that phone call.

Hard bones of wood slats against my fatigued back.

I took X by the hand and led him inside to the guest bedroom, and the two of us lay down together on top of the crisp blue duvet, and sleep took me at last.

*

We woke in the same instant. Our limbs had fallen together in sleep. X was so still, so still, barely a breath; he felt heavy with concentration, and I was as light and free as smoke. We were disoriented for many long minutes, fascinated by the proximity of one another's skin. He had ended up, somehow, with an arm thrown over my body, long elegant golden hand flat upon the bed. My hand traced the shape of his, slowly. It had the shape of earth: these are the runnels that cut down the distant hillsides in crooked clefts, the contours of hill that bloom with color in the summer, that bleat with green in the dry times, oh X, the perfect elongated Bench of your hand, the shape of the world, the shape of the earth.

I stroked the back of your hand, X; my touch was as light as a moth's leg. My thumb passed over and between your fingers, and through the dry valley of the space between your rough knuckles, and back again, to tour the world of your beautiful still hand. And soon I was aware of your breathing, a steady, deep rhythm, slow. I thought, Has he fallen asleep again? But then I recognized from the Adam days the expectant tension of your body and the warmth of your mouth near my neck.

Kiss me. It has been so many years. Adam, walking through the weeds out past the transformer box with the grasshoppers scattering in the sun, turned to look at me. I saw the shadow of the water tower, a teacup in midair. Kiss me.

*

Nearly every summer afternoon over Rexburg a towering bank of clouds mirrored the brown of the earth. Nearly every summer afternoon I held my breath eager for the fire flash, the fast exhalation of light across the cloud face that covered the whole of the sky, that pressed me down against the earth under warm golden weight. And the smell in the air before the storm struck – petrichor, electrified dry dust taking the sacrament of rain. Salt, the sweat of our bodies mingled together, the smell of X's shoulder where I pressed my face to muffle my cry as he pulled away, cry because the momentary loss of him was sharp; but when he released himself it fell on my thigh hot and sudden as the touch of God and I laughed with the rapture of relief, and he fell beside me on the bed with a sigh like thunder, his leg kicking involuntarily, rocked by a rough wake. I sank into sleep again with a warm throb spreading across the base of my spine, and it stayed there so I felt it in my dreams.

I dreamed of great warm open spaces under

Garden of Eden

a blue sun in a sky clear of smoke, overflown with thousands and thousands of birds. The sound of their wings drowned out all other sounds, even the sound of God's voice; the sound of their wings was the sound of X's deep steady sleeping breath, inhale, exhale, my X.

3.

I was sore the next morning. The ache in my hips startled me. X laughed at the way I hobbled. He said I walked like a cowboy.

"Well, it's your fault."

"Yee haw."

We ate apples in my kitchen and kissed the juice from each other's mouths. It was Saturday; James would be home this evening, and I would have to face my infidelity straight on. And X had already been in Rexburg for days.

"I'm leaving on Tuesday," he said. "Heading to Yellowstone." "Oh." Tuesday was cruelly close.

"If you want, you can come with me."

"I'm not sure I can do that."

"Why not?"

"It's stupid, I know, considering last night. But at least I can keep this a secret. If I left, I couldn't keep anything quiet at all. The whole town would know I'd gone and they'd know why."

"Is that so bad? You don't even like it here.

Garden of Eden

You said you've had it."

"But it's the only home I've ever known. Everyone I love is in Rexburg. My family. What would I do? Just up and leave, and then what?"

"Find someplace you like. Find a job. You're educated. You could work."

"It's not as simple as that."

"You're right. It's not. It's damn hard. The world is crazy. The world is shit. And the world is full of magic. You deserve to see some of it. Come with me. It doesn't have to be forever. If you hate the world more than you hate Rexburg, you can always come back."

"I could never come back if I left that way." Never. I remembered sparks flying from the tire of Marsha's pickup, the timid way she moved, gathering her clothes. I had said nothing to her. Don't concern yourself with an adulterer.

"Then go somewhere else. Find a place where you can be alive. Maybe James will find a place where he can be alive, too."

James. He's what decided me. "I *should* leave. If I don't just go, James will never go either. He'll be stuck here forever, pretending."

"But you can't do it for him. Do it for yourself."

"It's for me, too. It is. I want to go. But I have

to talk to James first. I can't just leave without any explanation. Let me talk to James first."

X put his arms around me. He smelled like apple peel, fresh and smart. "All right. Talk to James. You have my number. I'll be waiting."

But only until Tuesday.

4.

When James came home, relaxed and happy and jingling his keys, I couldn't stand to be in the same room with him. Funny – two years of his weekends away and I never batted an eye. It had all been so easy to justify when it was just him getting what he needed, that thing I couldn't give him. Now that I'd found a need of my own, the whole arrangement was suddenly shameful.

I showered to avoid talking to him. I fixed dinner in silence with my hair still wet, set his plate on the table, took mine off to the spare bedroom. He tapped on the door, and I told him to come in, but the conversation I wanted to have was reluctant to start. Instead I deflected his attempts to find out what was wrong with tight, cold courtesy and denials, and hated myself for doing it.

Eventually he gave up and went to bed, looking frightened and frail. I could hear him putting dishes in the dishwasher, turning off the lights, letting the water run in the master bath upstairs while he brushed his teeth. I curled up in the bed that still smelled like X. My thoughts were all of James, of how he and I used to talk about our favorite books during those three brief hopeful months before we

Baptism for the Dead

married, leaning across the chipped white tabletop of a Dairy Queen booth, tending toward one another, laughing. I remember how fervently I'd said to myself, He makes you laugh and he loves books. What else do you need? What else? It will be okay. Just do it. It will be okay.

It was all a mirage, of course. All three months of laughter and ice cream, the certainty that we were doing the right thing. You chase a mirage long enough and sooner or later the sun sets, and fantasy settles back into the earth and the ripples calm and you are alone in the desert. That, or you die of thirst.

Sunday morning James let me sleep in late. A good thing, since I hadn't fallen asleep until just before sunrise. He opened the door tentatively and found me awake, the blue duvet pulled up around my face. He wore one of those sweater vests he loved with the long-sleeved crisply ironed white shirt beneath. The Official Uniform of the English Professor, we used to call it, and then we would laugh, back in the days when we did that sort of thing.

"Do you want your toast?" He made me toast every morning with orange juice. Every morning, as long as he wasn't in Idaho Falls.

"No."

"You okay?" No answer.

Garden of Eden

"Are you sick? Please tell me what's wrong."

"I'm going to stay home from church today."

He withdrew, looking profoundly upset, confused, looking like he might cry. I wished I could make myself run after him and take him in my arms, smooth his hair, tell him it would be all right, we would stay like this forever because what more do you need, no one would ever have to know about Idaho Falls or X or any of this.

A bird called outside, an emphatic lifting note. I remembered X's bird profile, his long sharp nose against the sky up on R Mountain. Up on R Mountain where he had kissed me the way James never could.

I did not move from the bed until well after James had left the house.

5.

"You haven't been yourself lately, so I called your Visiting Teachers. They're coming over with their husbands to give you a blessing." James in the kitchen, tall studious James with his arms folded and his shirt tucked in.

"I don't need a blessing, James." I need to talk to you. I need to tell you.

"Why would you refuse one?" Accusatory. Suspicious. "I don't know what's going on with you, but a blessing will help."

Hocus pocus, I refrain from saying.

Making sandwiches, setting them on a plate, still feeling the warm weight of X's body bearing down against mine, stirring up powdered lemonade in a crystal pitcher. Drop in a few ice cubes. Crack, crack. James vanishing upstairs into the bedroom where he'll stay until Katherine and Danae and their husbands arrive.

This was all a mirage, I want to call up the stairs to James. But I stand alone in my kitchen and say out loud to nobody, "The sun is setting."

They ring the doorbell. I open it promptly. We're smiles all around and "We missed you in church; James says you're not feeling so well."

Garden of Eden

Danae has large front teeth and acne scars and limp hair and a limp personality but she still managed to find a husband who bends her over their foot-board every night. She says, "Your house is so beautiful, I always think that whenever we come to see you, what a beautiful home. It's lovely." Lovely, lovely. "And what a view." The R on Our Mountain squints at us across the valley. It's turning orange in the sunset. How tiny and weak Rexburg looks from the top of that mountain, how puny our temple is on this nobody hill.

"Well, we brought our husbands," Katherine says in a low voice. We're in the kitchen now and she's running water in the sink so the men can't hear us whisper. "We brought our husbands and they prayed about it and they are ready to give you a blessing. You and James both if he wants...."

James joins us in the kitchen, puts his arm around my waist like he's supposed to, kisses the back of my neck, a formal gesture, a peace offering, a display of husbandly concern for Katherine's benefit. I shiver and stop myself from pulling away. That is not my place, to rebuff my husband.

"I think you should," he tells me. "You need guidance right now. I don't know what's eating at you, but whatever it is, the Lord can help."

Baptism for the Dead

The pleasantries are over and nobody has really touched the sandwiches or the lemonade. Danae's husband, a man with a protruding gut and a loud laugh, pulls a chair away from the dark wood dining table and suddenly it's down to business. There were always too many chairs at that table, a futile anticipation of the children to come, three boys and four girls maybe and all of them with scrubbed faces and nice shoes on a Sunday night while I carry in the pot roast from the kitchen, James sipping a 7-Up with this trouser socks pulled up so neatly, feet crossed on the footrest of the La-Z-Boy.

Our children are waiting to be called over from beyond the Veil and

What the hells' the Veil anyway, X says, interrupting the scene. Or his voice, anyway; X is not here at all, of course, except in my imagination, where he is bare-skinned and vivid and breathing.

I try to define it for him inside my head where he can hear me.

Like the border between Heaven and Earth? Even my thoughts have a question mark at the end.

Oh, come on. Slow honey-voice, dark honey-voice, X.

Garden of Eden

I sit in the proffered chair. What else can I do?

The men lay their right hands on my head, left hands on each other's shoulders. I fold my arms and close my eyes, just like they taught me in Sunday school. Reverent. Katherine and Danae sit on the loveseat with the subtle floral pattern and are likewise reverent. James haunts the living room, too intimidated to participate. I open my eyes to look at him, his strained pale face; we catch each other's eyes and we both blush and I close my eyes again.

And it begins.

"I bestow on you this blessing, that it may guide and comfort you in your turmoil. (*Turmoil*, I like that.) You are God's beloved daughter, and He knows your heart. Know that God has a divine plan for you, that He guides you, that He sees you and loves you.

"Even your suffering and confusion are part of God's plan. You will be rewarded, not only in Heaven, but on Earth, with peace and the blessings of the family. God knows you will be strong and bear this burden.

"He wants you to know that He is proud of you, that you have great strength. Maintain your inner strength, turn to your sisters in the church when your spirit needs supporting, for in their righteousness they will uphold you.

Be open to the voice of the Holy Spirit – your life's calling will come soon. But you must be listening to hear the call.

"I say these things in the name of Jesus Christ, Amen."

When I open my eyes the sun has set, and James looks ill, the color all drained from around his mouth.

The men's hands leave my head. The awkward moment that always follows a blessing, when those who have delivered it wonder whether it was real, just for a heartbeat, before the zeal of having done God's work overtakes them again. The awkward moment that always follows a blessing, when the one who received it tries to perceive a change in her life, any noticeable effect.

And then the smiling, the tears of gratitude (Danae and Katherine, not me), the conversation that turns tactfully away from what we all just witnessed, and me listening for the call of the Holy Ghost with a contrary ear.

"Well, who wants brownies," I say, and everybody is relieved.

6.

Monday. Heat of day. Days growing warmer. Sun-touched flies along the verge of the road, bike chains ratcheting, Adam talking low and excited about...what?

X with his Adam eyes, one invisible in the depth of the pillow, watched as my head fell back in a tangle of hair. A kick of air leapt up from the bed with my movement, the smell of sweat and love and hotel room all mingling at once and subsiding.

"I'm going to do it," I told him. "I'm doing it for both of us – James and me."

"You're going to come away?"

"Yes."

"With me?" He sounded so glad.

"Yes. I have my own money saved up from the job I had during college. I can pay my own way." Without dipping into James's income. That seemed wrong. "I want to get out of here. What else is out there? I want to see it all."

"You'll love it all. I know you'll love it."

"And James – he needs to get out, too. This place will destroy him. He needs to go be who he is."

We stayed silent for a while. X's one visible eye filled me with some powerful emotion I could not quite place. I was following a sign into the wilderness. I was a blind pilgrim. I was afraid.

"How do you think he'll react?" I asked.

X thought about it. His eye closed. "I don't know," he said at last. "I hope he'll be happy about it, with time."

"Me too. I don't want to hurt him. I love him." When you love a man, you accept what he is. All of him, even the parts he can't show you. "Doesn't it bother you, that I still love James?"

"You wouldn't be who you are if you didn't love James."

"I'm not going to tell my family. I'm not even going to say I'm leaving. They'll find out everything anyway. It doesn't matter if I never tell anyone. Everybody will know." Silence.

"I'm going to do it tonight. Before I lose all my courage."

"Okay." Pause.

"Do you think he'll be okay, X?"

"I'm sure he will. It will take him some time to get used to it, that's all. Some day he'll thank you for it."

Garden of Eden

Once I'd decided, once I knew, X rose up to his knees, bent over me like a worshiper at some holy altar. His lips, tense as if to hold back a secret or a song, touched my left breast, my right, so lightly, pressed against my navel and twitched, grazed against my knee.

Afterward, when the day grew late and began to cool, just before the storm shuddered past the town, I got up from his bed and dressed to tend to my evening's task.

7.

When James ran out into the potato field I didn't quite know what to do.

The night as shot with stars, a big white spool of them unwound across the sky. I watched the stars near the horizon as I walked slowly after my husband. How many stars there are, how many. I tried to remember the names of all the constellations but...but nothing came to mind, just the elegant movement of X's hand, drawing. X was my tether to purpose. The memory of him in the golden light of the hotel lamp kept me fixed to my duty. Poor James.

The soil of the field broke beneath my feet. The plants slept in their orderly rows, optimistic leaves colorless in the night, ankle-high, their little white flowers just beginning to emerge, spreading a blanket of white on the earth all the way out to here the field met the dark distant mountains. Potato flowers bear no seeds. Imperfect flowers, they are called. But that night in the starlight they were at least beautiful, and their simplicity was a comfort.

Far ahead of me, James dropped to his knees. His crying voice rose up over rows of white. When I reached him I lowered myself to the ground. We knelt together in a furrow,

Garden of Eden

in a posture of prayer; I took him in my arms.

"It's okay." His head on my shoulder, sweet James who always smiled at me, who always had a joke to tell. James who looked about him so carefully at a world waiting to spring its traps. He cried. I held him tighter.

When I arrived home from X's hotel, James seemed inclined to settle in for a quiet night. But I had made up my mind to do what I had come to do.

"I don't know what I believe anymore," I had admitted to him. "But I know this isn't right, what this life does to you and me. It's not right and I don't want it. I don't want any of this anymore."

We had a bad argument. Bad. You just didn't bring it up around James, ever – what he was, his nature. If nobody ever talked about it, he could deny it, even to himself. He could deny it at least until he had to break away for a few days. Golf with the guys. Distantly, I knew I should be angry with him for not being strong enough to change. But my God, it's so hard to be angry with someone you pity. And if you knew him, truly knew who he was right down to the center of his soul, then you had to pity James, burned as he was by the hopeless weak sunshine of this life. Pity him, even though they all thought he was doing the right thing.

Baptism for the Dead

"It's okay," I told him.

We had fought, oh yes. He had screamed at me like a trapped animal for saying I would turn my back on the Church. His rage was terrifying, a part of him I had never seen before, my James who was always so carefully controlled. That blessing the men had given me was supposed to cure me of my pall. James didn't know what to do with a wife who wouldn't be cured.

And then I had told him, very calm, that I wanted to know his name – the man in Idaho Falls. Who was it he loved? Because I knew he didn't love me. The look on his face pulled me right off my feet, the fresh, awful wound in his eyes weakening my knees, taking my legs out from under me. But somehow I stayed standing straight and he was the one who buckled; he turned and ran.

He ran from the house, across the dark stillness of Poleline Road, over the ditch, out into the field. I followed him, thinking, What a beautiful night. There is nothing wrong here. We're making everything right.

James crouched in the soil. "I don't want to be like this. I just want to be normal."

"You are normal. This is what you are. This is how you were made."

Garden of Eden

"I want a normal life."

"But."

James caught his breath, choked and coughed, and smoothed his face with his hands, those neat beautiful hands. He was calmer when he said in a flat voice, "But I can't stay away from him. I know it's wrong, but I can't stay away."

I held his hand. I rubbed the backs of his fingers, gently, the way X had done to me when we held hands on R Mountain, alone above the valley. "Maybe you shouldn't stay away. Maybe it's better for you to be with him."

"Don't say that. I can't stand to hear that. Don't you think I've thought that a million times before? I love you; I don't want to leave you."

"Oh, James, I love you too. I do. I'll always love you. But you don't love me the way you love him. You know that's the truth."

The field was so quiet. The night was so cold. Cold nights are good for potatoes; the white blossoms nodded in a brief, brisk wind. James shivered.

"His name is Brian."

"Oh."

"I'm sorry. I've been unfaithful. I'm so, so

sorry."

I thought about it for a minute. I rubbed the back of his hand as if it was a good-luck charm.

Finally I said, "It's all right. Really. It's all right with me. I forgive you."

This was the wrong thing to say. James tore his hand from my fingers and groaned, pressed the heels of his hands against his eyes. "No. You can't forgive me. You can't just be okay with this. No one can forgive me. It's wrong to cheat and it's wrong for me to be...like this."

"I don't like that you cheated. But I forgive you. I understand why you did it. You love him." "I love *you*. You're my *wife*."

"I know you love me, James. But I'm a woman. I'm not Brian."

"Please don't say his name." He whispered this; his voice cracked; it was barely there at all.

"I don't see why you should keep him a secret. Love isn't anything to be ashamed of." I could feel James holding his breath, fearful. "Brian!" I shouted. The potatoes stirred. "He's nothing to be ashamed of."

James stared at me. I had never seen his eyes so wild, so intense. "Are you crazy? *This...*"

he hit his chest with a fist, hard, right over the heart "...is wrong. It's immoral. It's *bad*. This isn't love; it's disgusting."

"I don't want you to say that ever again. I don't care what everybody in town thinks. I don't care what the Church things. The Church isn't the whole world, you know. There are other churches out there. There are other people out there. There are people who don't even care about God, who don't believe."

"I'm not just *this*." And now there was a shocking potency in his voice, real conviction. I had never heard his voice do this before, rise up with such vigor and confidence. His voice was a tower. "I'm a husband, and a professor, and a member of the Church. I'm all those things at the same time. Do you know what it's like to juggle all those things? I've tried to find some balance in who I am my whole life. I can't just overturn everything to go off chasing some man because it *feels good*."

Yes, James, I know what it's like to hide. Mimicry, disguise, disruptive...I know. "He's not just some man. He's Brian. He's more than just some man."

I waited for him to speak. The ground was so cold. The chill crept through my jeans and pressed itself into my knees, my shins. But I held still, kneeling and waiting for James to speak.

"I met him in college," he said at last, defeated. "He was the first person I'd ever met who understood what it was like to be me. Because he was the same. Same story, same experience."

"You've been with him ever since college?"

"No. We were just good friends for a long time. We only...we only started *that* when I moved to

Rexburg to take my job."

"Oh." When he met me. Funny, that it hurt to hear those words, even for a moment, when I'd already made up my mind to forgive and cut us both free. Still, it touched up the memory of our sweet three-month courtship with a sour aftertaste. "What did he think, when you married me?"

James's laugh was bitter. "He hated it. By then he'd given up on the Church." He fell silent. His breath was barely visible in the starlight, a faint wisp of vapor. "He's always tried to get me to go along with him, to give it all up. But I just can't. It's a part of me. I can't turn my back on my life."

"It's why you married me. Because the Church is the biggest part of you." I had known all along, ever since our wedding night – before

Garden of Eden

then, if I am honest with myself – but the fact of it still hurt. No matter how rational I was, no matter how generously I had resolved to act, there was still a part of my heart that was wounded. I was still a woman discarded.

"I married you," he said firmly, "because I love you."

"You love me like you love your sisters. Like you love your friends. And that is honest love, I know. But you don't love me like you love Brian."

I half expected him to make some defense, or at least an objection. But instead: "I can't marry

Brian."

We both waited for the other to speak. The sky shouted with stars.

"You would if you could."

Far out in the field, the great long bracketed framework of the irritation system settled, creaking. It was a lonely sound, a sound with finality.

"Yes. If it was *right*, I would."

"Who decides what's right for you, if not you, yourself?"

"God." He drew the word out, fearful, high-voiced, a child's voice in the dark. James, my good husband, I loved you so much that I couldn't bear to see this shame on you anymore.

I stood. My knees ached with the cold. I felt the sting of the pavement summers and summers

ago, saw Adam picking his shirt up from the sidewalk.

"That's bullshit."

"Honey, come on. You don't need to…"

"Yes I do. I need to say it and you need to hear it. It's all bullshit." Adam! I never knew what it meant to say words like these so sharp and fierce until the spit flew from my mouth. I reeled from the power of my own words, and they came louder and harder. "If you believe in God, then you must believe that He made you the way you are. He had a reason for making you this way. It's men who have made you *wrong*."

"Stop it. You can't talk that way."

"What way?"

"Like you don't believe. Like I'm the only one who believes."

"I can't believe in this. Not this. You're not the only one who's affected, you know. Look at the life I've had to live, pretending I've got a real relationship with a man who really loves me. Because that's what's *right*. That's what they all expect of us. I don't care anymore what they expect. I need to be who I really am. And so do you."

"Don't do this."

"Stand up, James." He stared at me, wide-eyed, his breath a startled puff of pale blue. "Stand up."

He stood. My voice a crane. He stood.

I took him in my arms. The way my head fit just under his chin, the warmth of his familiar arms around me, the solidity of his back with its two identical bars of half-toned muscle. I concentrated on the feel of his back under my palms. This was our last moment together, I knew it – our last moment as husband and wife. I was about to kick his safe illusion all to pieces. I breathed deep to firm my resolve, and I smelled his soap, his aftershave very faint and fleeting, the smell of our home embedded in his sweater. *You have such a lovely home, I always think that.* James and me, lovely.

"I'm done. I'm not doing this anymore. You're not doing this anymore."

"No."

"I'm going to go away for a while. I need to get out of Rexburg until I can figure out where to go next."

Baptism for the Dead

"No."

"I think you should get out, too. Go spend the rest of the summer with Brian."

"Please. Please don't do this. God, please, don't let her do this."

"Go be in love for the rest of the summer, James. You deserve it. You need it. So do I."

"But my job is here."

"Not in the summer. You're off all quarter."

"And our house...."

"We'll figure out what to do about it when we've spent some time apart."

"Please don't do this. This isn't what I want."

I pulled away from him. The little imperfect flowers shivered all around us, all the way out past the endless web of irrigation pipes, out to the place where the Bench fell off the edge of the world.

"You'll thank me for it later. I promise you will. Go be in love. Please."

Hand in hand, both of us weeping, we stumbled back across the rows of silent plants, back toward the even squares of light across the empty road. Lights on in all the houses – families saying their prayers, getting ready for bed. One of those identical squares of light was

Garden of Eden

our house, the lamp we left burning. Inside, our home was lovely and warm and pulling away from us, vanishing on an unreachable horizon.

In our bedroom, we undressed and climbed under our comforter, and held each other, naked and innocent and familiar, until sunrise.

8.

The roads in Rexburg are too wide. I had always thought so, but never realized I had always thought so until I was leaving.

This Space for Lease in white shoe paint flaked off a window across from the hotel.

James and X nodded to each other, suspicious, territorial, cautious faces neutral for my sake. They broke off a curt handshake quickly.

I hugged James one last time, held him to me long, with equal measures of fear and relicf. "I'm going to pray," he said. "I'll pray for you too."

I nodded. "That will be good for you. To pray."

Cars passed, chiropractors and professors. Their obedient polished wives in the passenger seats watched James and his wife hugging outside the Best Western, sped by the brief flash tableau, and then back to musing over dinner. Pork loin. Roast chicken. Almondine.

James and I promised to call each other. He promised to head straight for Brian and Idaho Falls. He promised to enjoy his summer, but there was a heaviness in his eyes and I knew it would be harder for him than I had hoped. I

Garden of Eden

couldn't regret this. This was for him as much as for me.

X's portfolios and boxes and bags were stacked neatly in the back of his SUV, the dust-colored hybrid. He took my bags and settled them among his own, where their shapes and textures agreed.

The engine vibrated lightly.

Then there as the buckling in, the shifting about in the unfamiliar car seat, the adjusting of air and radio. And the backing out, and my eyes stinging at the sight of James turning resolutely away from me, ducking back into our sedan; the dizzy spin of the planted sidewalks as X wheeled his car around, pulled out onto the too-big road, accelerated past the Circle K, the pie shop, the tire store.

What were they thinking, the men who laid these roads so wide? They must have pictured a great tide of humanity rolling forth to fill the world with Truth, a migration of young men with neat hair and young women with fertile wombs who would spread the city limits out across the sage flats, out to the mountains, the march of an empire of Saints. What they did not envision was this: the trickling way of husbands and wives, two at a time, broken, in separate cars.

X and I, we drove down those roads as flat

and empty as made beds. We merged onto the Thirty-Three with a purr and a burst of speed, the highway which draws out to Sugar City and the mysterious hot dry places where the water sinks into the earth. The Thirty-Three and Sugar City, and on and on, away from this place.

Ghost cars. Full of the men who built Rexburg, who laid the roads too wide, who thought their labor could fix it all, the broken couples, the silence of God, the nakedness of art. Their wheels blurred, slow-motion – perfect children and moms in their aprons, dreams dissolving into smoke over the valley, hot with the smell of sagebrush, the movement of the scrub land in the wind, color-reversed, scattering,

...just before the dreamer wakes.

The Lone and Dreary World

The Lone and Dreary World

1.

Miles from Rexburg, over an inviting soft curve of wheat-planted plateau, the Tetons quietly assumed dominance over the landscape, and we stopped for breakfast in Driggs. The town as a friendly cluster of buildings ranked up around the highway, just after the road turned south and just before it fell down the pass into Jackson Hole. A huge faded fiberglass buffalo perched atop an empty stone diner with castle crenelations. A drive-in movie screen backed with gray weathered planks, maybe the last one in all the world, stood as timeless as an obelisk among the olive-gray scrub, and outside the drivein an enormous replica of a russet potato rested on the flat bed of a cherry-red snub-nosed truck. Cowboy Sized Omelet that X and I couldn't finish between us. Driggs was all monument and stillness. Even the Tetons obliged the theme; they rose straight up from the valley floor without the common courtesy of foothills, arrogant as statues, a cloak of cloud halted halfway through the act of sliding from the highest peak.

There was a bottomless pot of coffee in our diner, something practically unheard of in Rexburgian establishments. X made liberal use of it; the waitress kept pouring into his rustic blue tin mug and he kept emptying little top-hats of creamer, stacking them one inside the other with their foil lids peeled askew.

"Want some coffee?" he said.

I had never tried it before. Mormons, of course, are not sweet on strong drink and in my days of disguise I had done my best to look like one of them. But now that I was presenting a new sort of plumage to the world I figured there was no harm in a taste. It was awful. X laughed at the face I made and drained the last of his cup in a long draft.

When the tab was paid we climbed back in the car. It had become stifling inside as the morning grew late. X said it would only take a couple of hours to get to Yellowstone; we might as well explore a little. He like Driggs and wanted to see what else there was to it. We set out to find an inspiring vista.

Long empty green-scented roads divided fields of crop and pasture in a neat grid, each big square bordered by tall grasses with jagged seed heads moving frantically in the wind of our passage. Flocks of blackbirds burst from these wild verges at intervals to scatter across the road moments before the car could strike them from the air. We came to one juncture of road after another, and X turned the wheel this way or that, no agenda, no destination,

The Lone and Dreary World

wandering past post fences and barbed wire fences and acres with no fencing at all, just very rich, very green ditches wet with broad-leafed weeds, and out in the fields a quiet expectant placidity, the land waiting to be shown what to do. The lazy progress of the countryside on the heels of my dramatic morning made me sleepy. And that was to say nothing of the omelet. I laid my seat back and was about to tell X I thought I might take a nap when he slowed the car and said, "Look at that."

A mile or more ahead, the faded yellow block of some lone structure rose from a field, a dim upward slash against the bright grass. As we drew nearer the indistinct shapes resolved into a clearer scene. It was a house, old and long-abandoned but not quite a relic, two stories, painted yellow, most of its window panes still intact. A great cottonwood, large and ancient enough to have shaded the entire structure, had been uprooted by some unimaginable storm and now rested most of the way through the second story, cleaving the roof neatly down the center. What kind of wind could have felled such a tree? The thought of it chilled me. It must have torn through the valley like God's fist. The scene was all the more awful against the serenity of the field, the warmth of the June day, the heedlessness of the grown-over double-rutted trail winding out into the tall grass beyond the dirt driveway where X put

Baptism for the Dead

his car into park. We left the engine silently running, left the doors open – a wary bird ready to fly.

Neither of us was entirely willing to approach, yet still we were both drawn to the broken old homestead. Something about ruination attracts the human mind in a special, terrible way: train wrecks and car wrecks and celebrity divorces in tabloid magazines. There was no one else for miles around, no one else to bear witness, and the weight of awe fell on us alone. X was braver than I. He crept toward the house, two or three slow steps at a time and pause, as if he half-expected he might be turned to a pillar of salt if he came too near. When he made it to the house's dulled siding, put out a slow hand to touch, and survived, I strode after him, practically running, eager to close the distance between us.

An empty door frame yawned above pale porch steps. Bird droppings on the stairs. The beginning of a name spray-painted and abandoned, incomplete. The birdsong seemed tense and furtive. The sound of the roof cracking and the children crying in fear still wavered among the wheat. X peered into windows, paced around the perimeter, gazed up at the leafless, still branches. "Maybe I'll paint it," he said uncertainly.

I wanted to object to the idea of staying in

The Lone and Dreary World

this place long enough for him to complete even a sketch, but the ruin kept me silent. X approached one broken-out window, leaned partway in, looked around quickly. He seemed relieved to withdraw again. Then he stopped, glanced back inside, and said in a voice rough with pity, "Oh, no."

I was at his side in an instant. My own steadiness surprised me as I, too, leaned over the window frame. Walls intact, paper peeling to reveal the sickly yellow adhesive inside. Old carpet mildewed on the floor. The room reached back into the sun and shadow of the house's broken interior, met a hallway at a sharp corner where a fractional glint of an unbroken mirror still hung on a dull wall. I did not see what had upset X until I, too, began to turn away. And then, amid a tangle of thin rusted springs and rotting fabric that had once been a sofa, there was a huddled furry shape, dark, dry, and very still.

I stared for a long time before the particulate impressions (outstretched leg, long clean bare skull, sharp teeth) merged into a single, identifiable image: dead dog on the floor of the house. Small black dog with medium-long hair, face all gone, skull exposed, dull fur shedding away from the place on the haunch where sun streaming through the broken window for months or years had bleached the black to red. From the poor neck a long orange twist of bailing twine ran and disappeared amid the tangle of the old sofa.

"God," I whispered, and shivered.

"Who did this to you, little guy?" X said quietly. The dog said nothing.

"He was probably sick or hurt," I said. "Just crawled in here to die." And the bailing twine around his neck – broke off some dog house somewhere, not used to strangle him, not that. Sick or injured animals often took themselves away to die.

Such a wave of remorse and fear rose up over me that I had to put out a hand and catch myself against the siding. It was warm from the sun. I closed my eyes, and in the sharp purple light – the reverse echo of the house's innocent yellow – all I could see was James kneeling, crying in the potato field.

X raised his camera. It double-beeped on the focus and emitted its little electronic whir of shutter opening and closing. The birdsong in the field ceased for an instant, then resumed to fill the silence like an interrupted hymn.

2.

Grand Teton National Park: lush flowering meadows, scenic lake reflections, World's Most Photographed Barn surrounded by tripods and squinting cameramen, X slipping his lanky body in among them to snap a few shots of his own before turning back to wave at me, grinning. We paused to appreciate the midday glow of a mountain meadow backed by aspens, but the specter of the dead dog was still haunting me, and I'm afraid I took in the scene with only half a heart.

The rest of our drive that day was, I am sorry to say, a blur. It as undoubtedly a beautiful blur. There is no place half as poetic as the Grand Tetons in summer; if any place on Earth can unmake a nonbeliever, this is it. The starkness of granite, the delicate blush of alpenglow, and eastward, the great unrolling of the low grass valley, restless with pronghorns...and all this I know from later visits. When X and I passed by the range that summer I was in no fit mood to notice the grandeur of my surroundings. All my thoughts were for the spectacular wreck I had just made of my husband's life and mine. I was afraid my absence might destroy him, yet now I could never stop what I had started. And I wasn't certain I would stop it, even if I could.

Baptism for the Dead

No explanation for my behavior would satisfy Rexburg's ever-revolving gossip circles, those merry-go-rounds of good clean rural fun. My mother would eventually call me, and I would have to tell her where I was, and why. Then my sister and brothers would get the news, and before long Katherine and Danae would know all about it. Once those two had the rumor in their teeth it would be all over town, the whispered secret subject of every Relief Society meeting.

The knowledge that this would happen, its enormous inevitability, gave me a nonstop feeling of damp shivery illness. Because in spite of what I had told James that night in the potato field, Rexburg's opinion did matter. Save X, everyone I had ever known was in that town. I could not picture a life that didn't revolve around my community, assuming I could still call it my community at all. Yet what else did I have? An artist I had met only days before, the interior of his car, and the shifting crowds at scenic overlooks and highway rest stops. I had obliterated my place in the world, made myself homeless, for the sake of a man's body in a succession of hotel-room beds. That was the really amazing part. How unMormon of me, how *bad*. True, this was not any man – this was the lost love of my childhood come again – this was a *sign* – but even factoring Adam into the equation, the entire thing was

The Lone and Dreary World

too stupendous to be believed. The knowledge that I was capable of such brashness terrified and excited me by turns. One did not simply return to Rexburg after an adulterous cross-country escapade with a strange, beerdrinking, beard-wearing man. There could be no more business as usual, no picking up where I'd left off with meatloaves and Jell-O salads. In spite of having lived my entire post-Adam life trying to be perfect, a saint among Saints, somehow I had still engineered my own fall from grace, and I had done it all with as little effort as it took to pack my bags.

That I was capable of this ruinous impulsivity stunned me. I wavered queasily between two extremes of self-image. On the one hand, I felt great pride in my confidence – what a polite Mormon woman might call "inner strength" and what X might call "having balls." On the other hand, I was tormented by my fear of a bleak, rootless future where, without the simple wholesome sameness of my hometown as lodestar, I would drift among worlds of dust and rust inhabited by dissatisfied shades, where I would be forever without connection, without direction, without happiness.

The memory of the dog's pathetic shape among the wreck of the house made my guts tight with anxiety. If X was a sign, then so, surely, was the dog. There was a way life was just *supposed to be*, forms to be followed, conventions to be observed. And the payoff for perfection was true contentment, a happy life. I had cracked my own roof right in two, and now there would be more sad lost things strangling inside me than I could ever count.

The irony was not lost one me, that it was only when I had left Rexburg that I'd come to doubt my doubt. As X ecstatically painted, standing among knee-high grasses with a mist of sage flies wavering about him, I stared into the stern faces of the Tetons, all hard angles and cold indigo planes, as near and imposing as a temple, and I wondered whether I was really as alone and unaccountable as I had thought.

X, you don't know how different I was with you, how un-Mormon, because you never knew me before. When you watched me toss my temple garments onto your chair did you understand what you were seeing? You were witness to a terrible transformation, an intense golden fire of metamorphosis that burned away something original and deep, something wrapped and protected. Mine was not the gentle emerging of a butterfly from its cocoon. Your body, X, your voice, your hands, your goddamn sketch pad – you were the brush fire that cracks the chrysalis as it hangs mute from its dry stem. You made me remake myself, and the scars of my remaking will always burn.

There is this ember inside of me, an animal

red, an awful crimson. No matter how I try to smother it, it continues to glow.

Do you know, X? Do you know how I am crippled, how even a God I don't believe in still has the power to rub the scales from my wings, how even when I am with you I can still feel that miserable brand inside me, smoking, and how sometimes I wish I did believe, just for the simplicity of it, for the ease of knowing that to want you and to have you is wrong, absolutely, unmistakably, simply – even though it feels as right as breathing.

We made Yellowstone by sunset – do you remember? – and by the time we had checked into our hotel the stars were emerging from a violet, pine-scented sky. In our lodge room I opened the slats of the blinds until the mild light of night-time streamed inside and touched us, touched you as you pulled me against your bare chest and held me there to comfort me. The blinds made on the nearest bed a pattern of starlight and shadow that broke and misaligned and flowed, light into shadow, like the ridges of a thumbprint. Do you remember how the starlight fell across my back when I undressed, across the cool bed where we lay, where our breath caught and merged like smoke, how seconds moved like ages as slow as stone? Do you remember, X, how all that was real was rhythm and stars and skin?

3.

I had a terrible dream. A tree fell through the roof of our lodge, trapped us inside. I picked up the hotel phone to call for help, but a tinny recorded voice recited scripture at me, endlessly, in polite monotone, and offered me a selection of buttons to push for help. I mashed the keypad with a paw-like hand but nothing happened. The voice went on and on where it had left off, and finally, sensing that no help would ever come, X with a horrible feral grin put a length of bailing twine around my neck and tightened it, and I woke, gasping and trembling, while X muttered beside me in his sleep, his mouth slack and peaceful.

I got up from our hotel bed and turned on the tap – its pipes groaned and grated for an instant but X did not stir. I drank flat, warm water from my cupped hands, and told myself, I've lost all the meaning in dreams. The significant has become the insignificant, mere coincidence or biology. What had been a signpost or a clue from on high was now the sorting and parsing of my own overstressed mind, its colorful attempt to categorize the various horrors of life, to set order to a burst of awful image and emotion so that it – I – could understand. What else could a dream

The Lone and Dreary World

be? What else made sense? Nothing. I went through this litany several times until I was partially reassured, until the inborn

Mormon awe and terror at having witnessed another sign faded a little, and I could yawn again.

I crept back into bed and pressed myself against X's side. His breathing was easy and soft, automatic. Life goes on without direction, without any cosmic neon arrow pointing the way. As I lay there feeling X's warmth and weight I considered whether it was better this way, with everything ultimately meaning nothing. At least with God in the picture nightmares could be turned into warnings. Wasn't the illusion of control preferable to the fact of...of whatever was really fact?

I could not get back to sleep. Long before X woke, I slipped outside and wandered around the lodge's parking lot among dirt-faded cars bearing bug-crusted bumpers and foreign license plates. Between the last of the night's stars and the oncoming sunrise, pale pink somewhere in the mountainous east, there was sufficient light to see where I was going.

The sharpness of my anxiety made everything seem more significant and agonizing than it really was, even if there was no watching God to lend a special meaning to that agony.

Baptism for the Dead

As I paced between Nebraskan sedans and New Mexican vans the whole arrangement of space and time and parking lot and dawn light underscored the frail loveliness of life. I felt the lodge and all its travelers tucked away inside, X with his watercolors and his wide boyish grin, far-off James in his sweater smelling of home, all shivering at once along the surface of my tense tired body, a unison note, the whole beautiful burden reverberating like a struck tuning fork inside my veins. How pretty we all were, everything was – and how spectacularly pointless, too, as here we lay, snuggled together in the huge hollow eye of a volcano, which could blink at any second and turn the whole works into a puff of hot steam.

I was in that kind of mood. On reflection it was probably not the best mood for phone calls. But all the same, I haunted the parking lot with my cell phone in hand, searching for any small patch of ground that would grant me a bar or two of signal. At last I got it, and dialed James's number. He answered just before his voice mail did. He did not sound sleepy, despite the early hour. I had not wakened him. I guessed he hadn't slept the night before. All well and good; neither had I. Not much.

"Did you make it into Idaho Falls all right?" Awkward. Awkward conversation. How do you talk to your husband who is lying in bed with his boyfriend?

He affirmed, a little coldly, a little confused. Everything was all right. He was upset still, but listen, he guessed he'd be okay. Was I okay? Where was I?

"Yellowstone. We got here last night." Silence. If I knew my James, he didn't like the sound of *we*. "There's not much signal here, so I might lose you."

"What do you care if you lose me anyway?"

"Come on, don't be like that. I know this is hard on you, but don't you think this will be better for both of us?"

"No. I don't think this will be better for either of us, and I still can't believe you're doing this to me. I thought you were a better person than this."

"I don't want to hurt you, James. I just want us both to be happy."

We exchanged a few more chilly sentences. He made some attempts at making me feel guilty, which mostly worked. I said good-bye before he could turn the conversation into a fight. There was a nasty hard thing in my stomach, painful, the sharp pit of a sour fruit.

I did not go back inside immediately. I found X's big dusty hybrid and climbed up onto its hood. The metal was cold enough to make me shiver. I laid my back against the slope of the windshield and watched the glow deepen in the eastern sky. I was still vibrationally aware of my place in nature; my place in un-nature, too – even the coldness and hardness of the car seemed significant, and its hollowness. An angry rasping bird called from the thin pine trees across the parking lot. Its voice was nasal. I felt the call grating inside my own head, but I didn't mind. The bird and I were plucking strings of the same chord.

Once, when I was a very little girl, I had believed that a caring God had made everything for me, for me and for everybody, and that He had nothing better to do with His eternity than watch and rejoice as we rejoiced in His Creation. He had a great book of parchment papers with a cracked old leather cover and binding, and in it was written everything that would ever happen: the day a little girl in a sunlit field would discover the delicate way a ladybug's glassine wings emerged from its candy carapace, the symmetry of its four wings spread, the dramatic pause just before it lifted into flight, an orange blur trailing a wake of childish laughter. The day a little girl would learn that she loved the scent of rain in the sagebrush, that it was as right and real to her as the feel of bricks in the church wall. The day a girl would sit alone on a car in a parking

The Lone and Dreary World

lot and feel a bird call inside her chest, and feel a man cry inside her chest, and feel the precarious stirring of the earth, and would love it all because it was all life, and all real, and all hers to rejoice in. And God would rejoice with her, because He had made it all for her.

I miss that feeling. I long for the simple comfort of myth, the warmth of the blanket tucked up to my chin in the night, the nightlight glowing. I still want to be the innocent heart that can truly believe that His eye is on the sparrow and the ladybug and me.

4.

The bird calling in the pines, the vibration of nature. The last time I felt that way, the deep awareness of the world that made me almost sick with its relevance, I had been a girl in Rexburg, reeling from the fresh loss of Adam.

The new school year after that windy summer had begun. The park's birches had turned as golden as the fields surrounding the town, though like the fields, fleeting touches of green still clung doggedly and flashed here and there in the wind. The implicit tragedy of that failing summer color and its obvious parallel to my secret turmoil made me want to weep with understanding or bitterness or both. But if I had done so, my friends would have known I was hiding something, so I nursed my heartbreak in absolute, well-groomed silence.

Ever since I realized my fiery Bench-bound affair with Adam must be kept out of the hands of Katherine and her disciples *or else*, I had come to dread the skittish prim sex talks she always initiated. Katherine's interest in marriage and its requisite activities had been increasing every day, fanning itself into a barely restrained frenzy. In spite of her rampant hormones she was careful to set a good example for the rest of us girls, and always steered our little conversational dinghy just so, skirting the reefs of out-and-out lust where we were all in danger of wrecking and despoiling. Yet she couldnt leave the subject alone. She always managed to bring it up one way or another, sitting in the grass at the park, arranging her lovely tanned teenage legs in just the right way to suggest sweetness and modesty, or over milkshakes in a corner booth, whispering and twisting a plastic straw around her ring finger. She poked at the subject of sex relentlessly, professional and fascinated, a junior gynecologist. Inevitably, after encouraging our talk, Katherine would let the giggles and puns swell and flush, and then she would douse the whole antsy conflagration with a reminder that *all that sort of thing* wouldn't be any fun anyway unless it was done after one's wedding, with one's ordained husband, to whom one had been sealed in the temple for time and eternity.

Oh yeah? I'd think with a plaintive pang, watching the leaves shiver in the dying wind.

She was the same age as the rest of us, but something about Katherine – her prettiness? Her perfection? – commanded a greater share of respect and deference than we gave to anybody else. Secret love lives aside, we were all good Mormon girls, cut from the same sturdy, clean, handsome if unembellished cloth. Yet

Baptism for the Dead

God or nature had put a little extra twist in the fabric of Katherine, a little extra sheen. She stood out. All of us wanted to be her. She had a straight bright smile, academic success, hair that was flawlessly, freakishly smooth and golden, and a knowledge of scripture that was both encyclopedic and intimidating. Her skin was always glowing, her pores always invisible. When she entered the school gym or the parched flat ball field in her crew-neck t-shirts, her small breasts and thin legs looking all the more sensual for the unconsciously modest way she clothed them, the boys all watched Katherine to the exclusion of everything else around them – flying basketballs, looming fence posts, speeding trains. She held sway over the girls as easily as she did those poor awkward boys. Silently, from the outer edge of the group, I would watch Katherine take control of a perfectly pleasant conversation and prod it just to the edge of badness, then reel it back in so deftly and demurely, and every time I would think that Katherine could be free of the lust that plagued her if she would just give in and have a good roll in the weeds with some boy from our grade.

She would wax ecstatic over the bliss that awaited us all after our temple marriages. I would feel smug, illuminated, wise, because I already knew that fumbling bliss. And I would feel guilty, because by pursuing my lusts I had

The Lone and Dreary World

altered my path forever, had denied myself the life that pure Katherine had earned: peaceful and unchallenging and well delineated, if not strictly *blessed* by a God I could not understand.

I often wonder whether those flighty conversations during our younger days, all that time spent comparing my prospects to Katherine's, originated my nuisance ember of guilt. Even more maddening than its source is the question of why it still has the power to burn me, years later. It flares up from time to time like a bad case of indigestion, and I am embarrassed to admit this, because after all... well, after all, I am no believer.

Incidentally, I am not the only Rexburger, ex- or otherwise, who struggled with her relation to sex. All the women of the town – and the men, too, I suppose – kept a veil drawn tightly around their *celestial bliss* that felt more like defensiveness than politeness or modesty. Are amorous anxieties pandemic to eastern Idaho?

I have good evidence that even Katherine ran into trouble when she finally got her anticipated temple marriage to some returned missionary or other, a clean-cut, smiling boy like all the rest of them. She was the first of our group to marry. This fact surprised no one, as she was the prettiest young woman in town, the most charismatic, and the most impatient to become a wife. A few weeks after her honeymoon I invited her out for cupcakes and hot chocolate at the campus cafe, my treat. My ruse was to hear all about the manufactured romance resort in the Bahamas where she and her bewildered new husband had spent ten days getting sandy and tanned – and, one would assume, thoroughly acquainted. My true motive was to compare notes: to find out whether the marriage bed was the divine, Godapproved bliss Katherine had expected it to be, and whether I could discern any real difference between her experience and mine.

She had been happy enough to wax rapturous on the beauty of the islands, the azure warmth of the water, the attentive service of the resort staff. She showed me pictures on her little camera: beach vista with plantation of palm trees captured mid-sway, sunburned new husband on horseback, awkwardly handling reins in the surf. But when I gently coaxed the conversation toward the bedroom as she, smiling behind her hand, had done so often before, Katherine clammed up. I was almost embarrassed to see the panic in her eyes, the cloud layer of distaste. I had intruded into a place where even Katherine didn't want to go, and now I felt sorry. I chalked this up to first-timer's nerves and allowed her to change the subject.

The Lone and Dreary World

But it happened again, after Katherine's family was well established, when my own ill-fated marriage had just begun.

Our ward director had designated Katherine my Visiting Teacher – a sort of religious advisor/spy who made inconvenient house calls, prying into her charge's health, finances, state of emotional crisis. I had always found Visiting Teachers a bit violating. Didn't I get enough Church on Sundays? Privately, James and I referred to ours as the Visiting Creatures. We largely shirked our own home-teaching duties, sparing our charges unwanted midweek drop-ins, James on the excuse that he did enough teaching at work, thank you very much, and I on the excuse that I was generally no fun to be around and no help to anybody besides.

James and I were perhaps three or four months into our celestially ordained bliss, but there was no bliss to be had, and for once I was relieved and glad to see my Visiting Creature making her monthly trip down my walkway in her smart flats and modest capris. I welcomed Katherine with a genuine hug and a glass of lemonade.

We sat on the couch near the view window. We conversed. We laughed. We were young Mormon wives, and life and eternity spread out before us like a brightly colored, well-drawn map, lucky us, lucky us. How is your

Baptism for the Dead

baby, Katherine? Oh, he's such a little treasure, such a good boy. How is the college treating James? He loves his work; life is perfect, we are so blessed.

Soon enough, though, we wore out the call and response. A somewhat strained silence settled over my living room. I could hear the wall clock ticking in the foyer. I shook my glass gently. The ice cubes rattled. At last Katherine cleared her throat, and softly inquired as to the health of my marriage. It was the question I had been waiting for. James's nature may never have been a fit topic for conversation, but the town still knew, and Katherine had surely wondered how we were getting on. The moment the question was out of her mouth I opened a floodgate on my friend which I am afraid nearly drowned her. I confessed that James seemed to have little physical interest in me. When we did go to bed together the whole experience was awkward and impersonal. Certain crucial parts refused to work reliably. I despaired of ever having children. At the rate we were going, I said, I might become a mother somewhere around the age of sixty-five.

Katherine looked well beyond her depth, the poor thing, stupefied with her lemonade glass clutched in both hands. I realized as I unburdened myself all over her that in the act of camouflaging myself so carefully amidst the Rexburg milieu I had actually swallowed the

The Lone and Dreary World

party line, hook and all: marriage was supposed to change James. Once he had a wife, his life would take the shape he wanted it to have, like magic, like an endowment. But the proscribed cure was having no effect, and I felt cheated and dismayed, and raged on his behalf as much as my own.

Finally Katherine interrupted me. You just need more time. It takes a while to get to know each other; you can't expect to be comfortable with intimacy right away. Pray about it. Heavenly Father will open your hearts. I know he will.

"How long did it take you and your husband after you were first married? I mean, how long until it became...fun?"

Katherine's eyes went as dull and flat as old coins. But the smile stayed on her face, the precise perfect smile of the happy wife. "Well, it's wonderful now, of course. Wonderful."

What was this strange duality in Rexburg? What made Katherine, who was once so eager for a husband, deflect any questions of intimacy with that soulless plastic smile? What drove James to even *try* in our bed, for the short time he did try, when he longed for something I could never give him? Something about the town or the temple, the masks we all wore, kindled those fires and compassed us all with sparks, and all of us lay down in sorrow.

Baptism for the Dead

And why, even after I left, did that wretched guilt consume me? It smoldered inside me; it obscured the world with its sickening smoke. And how could I feel so splendidly alive, so awakened to the world, with the bird in the pine trees scolding inside my head, with the pines moving in the breeze of my pulse, with the sunrise coloring my skin and my skin coloring the sunrise, and yet feel so ashamed of you, X, of my love for you, which was the very thing that had finally made me live?

It wasn't fear of a vengeful God. Not on my part.

I set my face like a flint, but the shame still flooded me. So many questions still came. And no answers for me, or for anyone else.

The Lone and Dreary World

5.

Yellowstone was a strange stinking utopia of beautifully colored pools, the slap of hot water against calcified pillars, ghosts of steam rising from the earth to drift knee-high into the spread arms of our headlights (night drive), views of river rapids down a road's precipitous drop, and a single bison, right on the shore of Yellowstone Lake, black against an impossible June blue. We stood with the crowd to watch Old Faithful erupt, and the tourists oohed and aahed right on cue, and X kissed me and pulled me against him, and the wind blew that special geologic smell into our faces, ripe rich brimstone and choking heat, sulfur mist on our cheeks, X's mouth against my ear, a foreglimpse of the adulterer's very pleasant and very cheerful hell.

During those earliest days of our joy ride I bounced between two distinct poles. So long as we hiked some rocky trail thick with insects and the fresh smell of mountains, or took in a sunglowing mountain vista, or lay catching our breath in a hotel room, I could fade my guilt into any picturesque background that presented itself. I sat at picnic tables in park after park, pretending to read, watching X paint scene after scene on his blocks of watercolor paper, his sun-browned hands so big but so precise, and always I felt a warm reassurance, sunny, the vague but comforting idea that everything would eventually be okay, that I was having a good time after all, that all of us were on an adventure, even James.

It was when we took to the highway again that my dread returned. The monotony of long stretches of road, the grayness, the oppressive relentless tempo of telephone wires scooping and rising in passing, the black flash of their poles like heads in a congregation nodding – something about the repetition of travel wore down my defenses, so that I felt no awe for my inner strength anymore, only horror at my own stupidity.

X did what he could to distract me. He told stories and jokes. He sang songs. I was aware that I had an obligation to be a good travel mate, and I responded to his gestures with something I hoped looked like sincerity, or at least gratitude. I even taught him a song of my own, the day we left Yellowstone and headed east for points unplanned and unknown. It was a childhood song, sung in a very special, irreverent way.

Jesus wants me for a sunbeam, we sang. Only we rolled our windows down so we could shout the word *beam* at the top of our lungs.

The Lone and Dreary World

To shine for him each day.

It was the only rebellion Mormon children were ever allowed – a mutiny cry carefully modulated so as not to offend *too* much.

In every way try to please Him, at home, at school, at play.

A sunBEAM, a sunBEAM, Jesus wants me for a sunBEAM.

All those poor Sunday school teachers, gritting their teeth as their classrooms exploded on *beam*, delivered in a screech intended to shatter eardrums. But nobody ever banned the song. The teachers had sung it that way, too, back when they were children. In the very young something primal wants to push back. All those sweet darlings in their sweater vests and their crisp little dresses, singing of being so pleasing while they fired off that rifle report. You could tell which teachers had been the most defiant in their own days. Those sly grinning mommies allowed us to sing it every Sunday.

With X I sang and shouted along the straight stretch of highway, the wind pulling the word out over the grass, BEAM, where it made birds spring up from wire fences and range cattle flick their ears, but otherwise was as useless as it had been years ago within the walls of church classrooms.

Baptism for the Dead

Singing only kept me buoyed so long. The desolate empty grasslands kept pace with our car and seemed to groan at me in disapproval. The further we went into Wyoming's featureless prairie the heavier my sadness grew.

Evening came on and we were getting hungry. We found a motel in Gillette, a low, flat, grimy facsimile of my hometown. It was a colorless place with the clustered silhouettes of grain elevators indicating its halfhearted boundaries. A line of coal power plants smoked against a vast orange sunset, a wan industrialized specter of Rexburg's temple. Our motel shared a parking lot with a drug store; we raided its shelves for bottled juice, candy bars, trail mix, ultra-thin condoms. I thought sadly as I set our purchases on the cracked checkout counter, So this is what my life has come to. And then, in the parking lot, X took my hand in his as we walked toward our rented room. He sang a funny song that I suspect he'd made up on the spot, and without warning he spun me under his arm, around and around as if the parking lot were an elegant ballroom, and sad Gillette at dusk became a bright fairyland, all sunbeams and rainbows in spite of the coal dust obscuring everything. The gloom of the road fell away. An intense desire for him rose up, and I smiled at my X, the first real smile since leaving Rexburg. He grinned back with is big-toothed grin and his blue, blue eyes, and

The Lone and Dreary World

I thought, So this is what my life has come to. And there was never a time before, not at church, not at temple, when I had felt so grateful or, dare I say it, so blessed.

We moved on.

Rozet, nothing but a few manufactured homes standing in dreaming green fields overlaid with train tracks, traversed by bright-colored coal trains, mile-long dragons sluggish with fire. East. Devil's Tower, a stone temple where X painted for hours, standing at his French easel among tall grass and sage brush, brim of hat pulled down over his long nose, I dozing on a blanket spread on the grass, smelling of bug spray and sunscreen. I watched through a sleepy waver as he raised his arm to the square and measured, thumb against pencil, and shifted shape before my dozing eyes from a fourteenyear-old boy with thick, thick glasses to his present, attainable, infinitely more desirable state. He wore an old green apron over his jeans, splattered with paint, heavy with rags and brushes. On a dry bit of highway we sat in a traffic jam and watched a moose menace a blue Volkswagen. Spearfish, Sturgis, Rapid City, an intense sunset blood-red and blood-purple over an endless similarity of Badland buttes, nature's own Rexburg, all modest color and steeple. X and I pulled off the abandoned road. I climbed into

Baptism for the Dead

his seat, straddled his lap, and brushed with my tingling mouth the fine filament hairs over his bare shoulder, where the late Dakotan light rang like a drum against his warm skin. We went south through Porcupine and Wounded Knee, and made what we could of western Nebraska, of all its nameless towns with their identical silos, old-timey shop fronts along listless brown avenues, broken windmills in tangled fields, backdrop of Chimney Rock under a black anvil cloud.

Through all of this, through days of travel, I accustomed myself to the rhythm of the road. Call James in the morning, argue. The gloom of driving, brush-fires of remorse pursuing me in the clouded side-view mirror. And at night, on hotel beds that were unsatisfactory for sleep, in rooms that smelled of sage brush, old cigarettes, and recirculated air, the steep ascent into paradise, a margin of relief where I admitted nothing – not Rexburg, not James – nothing but the presence of X, the fact of him, his reality – and his unreality, too, the faint trace of Adam's smell, the only substantial thing in a mercifully formless void.

When we had finished and he was asleep with his back to me, covered by the thinness of a sheet, my eyes moved where my hands had moved, along the stark slanting line of his body, pale against the darkness of the room, peak of shoulder to hip, and in a haze I would wonder how even when we were still, even when we were done, how just lying beside him was enough to drive everything else from my mind.

The hotels were my only remedy. Each evening at check-in time I scrubbed away my anxiety with a new freshly unwrapped soap bar in a new lukewarm shower in a new nowhere town. Sometimes X would join me in my shower. He would wash my back for me, bend his neck to kiss me; there would be shower spray on his eyelashes and in the fine dark hairs of his eyebrows, sparkling like rain over the Bench. But when morning came my phone was in my hand again. James was in my ear again, pleading, accusing, and the whole awful routine began again the moment we took to that loathsome highway. I couldn't manage to keep myself confined to the easy spaces where X and I floated in our isolated sea. Every sunrise was a fresh reminder that I had no strength to break Rexburg's hold.

6.

A fire cannot rage in your heart but spare your clothing from burning. You cannot walk through a bonfire without blistering your feet. The burns will tell. The smoke will tell. The world will see how your lust smolders, and the world will despise you.

Adultery is wrong because it incites jealousy. It incites rage. It makes one man fight against another, and neither will ever be satisfied no matter how many blows are struck or how many wounds are dealt.

Adultery is wrong because God dictates matches and mating; because God chooses our partners and who are we, to think we know better than God? I hear Katherine's voice inside my head: *Well, who cares if I don't like going to bed with him? Who cares if it's not what I thought it would be? This is the husband God gave me, and who am I? Who am I to second-guess our Heavenly Father?*

It is wrong because theft is wrong, because what is given to one man is his to have, because all men despise a thief, because what is taken can never be repaid.

Oh, there was so much certainty before I met you, X. Wrong because everybody will know. Wrong because because this is all so

The Lone and Dreary World

simple, it's easy, it's as clear as day, and you can be certain that you're doing the right thing, always, all the time.

X and I sitting at the counter of a diner in Prairiesville, lacquered wood bar, hard chair anchored to the ground, tipping a little when I pivot the seat too far to the left. The woman behind the bar stabs a check onto an aluminum spike beside the register. She turns to us to take our order; her eyes are small and tired behind the drooping brown eyeliner that all older Catholic women wear; there is a tiny silver crucifix hanging around her neck. She smiles at us so kindly and says, after she notes our orders, "It's real nice to see two kids like you in love." The old man at the counter beside X stirs his coffee and grunts in agreement.

There is a great gout of flame in my heart, and a crackling of sparks, the snap of a twisted limb burning. There are bite marks on my shoulder and a message from my husband on my phone. Can't they see, the waitress and the old man? They are supposed to see. They are supposed to despise me. It's wrong,

because god says so

as simple as that as clear as that

7.

Nebraska morning. Pale yellow light over the empty parking lot beside the hotel. The tips of long grasses blazed. Across the highway a stand of shade trees stood well back from the road, sheltering a small white house at the end of a long dirt drive. I had excused myself to the parking lot, as I did every morning, for the ritual call. I could have called James in the private corners of hotel lobbies, at the ends of gray rooms where continental breakfasts were offered, my side of the conversation masked by the noise of travelers. I could have called him in the room, with X shaving his neck at the dimly lit sink. X wouldn't have minded, wouldn't have interfered. I preferred parking lots. There was always a road within view. There were always cars in motion, people going away. As James wept or railed in my ear I kept my eyes on the passing people. I reminded myself that I was one of them, traveling, working my roots free of hard yellow soil, soon this call would be over, I had done my duty to check in, soon I would be somewhere else, a new hotel, miles closer to figuring this mess out.

In the empty lot beside me the heads of yellow-framed, black-eyed flowers were just visible above the grass tips. Small brown birds dipped into the space where the flowers nodded, arcing low, snatching insects from the glowing air. I watched them for a time. I felt nothing for those few moments – no anxiety, no lust; I felt the alternating drop-and-rise, the stiff-feather beat of wings, the snick of wind against the falling small bodies. I preferred parking lots because they were as close to nature as I could get in the mornings.

In my pocket, my phone buzzed. I pulled it out quickly, relieved to see James's name on the screen, relieved as I always was when I spoke to him, reassured that he was still there.

"James?"

Silence. Just for a moment, silence – enough time for two birds to arc down into the field and rise again on quick wings.

"Hello, I'm sorry." Not my husband's voice. Higher in pitch, softer. "My name is Brian. I know we've never met. I'm...." He trailed off.

"You're James's boyfriend."

The man on the other line made a small noise, maybe a sigh, maybe a laugh. "Yes."

And then in an instant my heart lurched, my eyes filled with tears. "What's happened to James? Why are you calling on his phone?"

"I'm sorry. I didn't mean to upset you. James

is okay; he's at the store right now. I sent him out. But I wanted to talk to you. I didn't have your number, so I used his phone."

"Oh, God. I thought something had happened."

We laughed together, the quiet, polite chuckle of embarrassment.

"I'm worried about James," Brian admitted. "He's not taking this well." And he told me how James could hardly be roused from bed, how he cried, how when he was not crying he read scripture, underlining passages with emphatic strokes, biting his lips. How James didn't want to talk about me, and didn't want to talk about the future, either. "That scares me," Brian said. "He doesn't seem to care about the future at all. I'm afraid he'll try to hurt himself."

My heart, a sickened, hollow, small thing, strained in my chest. "I don't know what to do."

"I know. I'm not asking you to do anything."

"I should go back. I should get back to Rexburg and stay with James."

"No. I'm not in it anymore – the Church, I mean. I left."

"He told me about that."

"I am trying to get him to see, too, that it's

better to leave if you don't fit in. I think you did the right thing. He just needs more time."

"But what if he...?"

"He won't. I didn't want to worry you. I'm sorry. I guess...I guess I just needed to talk to somebody who understands. Somebody who loves him, too."

"I do. I do love him. I'm afraid I've hurt him too much by going."

"He'll be okay. I just needed to talk to somebody."

I told him I was glad he'd called, although I was not. I was trembling and cold. My stomach knotted up hard. I told him, "You can call me any time you need to talk. I'm always here. Just...please tell James...tell him it's going to be okay."

Fragments of Brian's words repeated in my head long after he had hung up. I watched the empty lot and listened to the broken echo. Future try to hurt himself somebody who loves him doesn't care about he'll be okay. My parking lot, my simulacrum of nature, was as hard and cold as the lines James inscribed beneath passages in his Book of Mormon, as uncomforting. The highway roared. I turned my back on it and crept back inside to watch X shave and pack. He asked me what was wrong.

I said, "Nothing. Nothing is wrong. He's going to be okay."

8.

With the justice of God, men shall be judged according to their works. And if their works are good, and the desires of their hearts are good, when the long night comes they shall be restored to that which is good. And if their works are evil, they shall be restored to evil.

All things restored to their proper order, everything to its natural frame. Mortality raised to immortality. Corruption raised to incorruption. Raised up, and raised up, according to my good works, up to endless happiness, up to inherit the Kingdom of God. All I have to do to get to the Kingdom is desire good, and do good. By grace am I saved, and by my works am I rewarded.

My reward is a place of comfort, a place of rest, a place where time has no meaning, no brevity, no urgency, no constraint. By my works and my desires will I reward myself with an endlessness of love and community, a family dressed all in white whose hands are always stretched out to catch me, though in such a place I could never fall.

We are gathered around the table, all of us in white robes that glow with the brilliance of joy. Our faces are clear and untroubled. Between us there stretches a web of perfect understanding, of clarity of sight. All the faces I love, all the hands that will catch me. The children I have yet to bear. My mother and my father. My sister and my brothers. And James and X and Brian and me, perfectly connected, perfectly loved, unending.

There are no walls to this place. It is a glow within a glow, where faces and hands stand out with breathtaking sharpness against the comfort of white on white on white. Layers of peace, the Veil behind which I have left the concerns of the world.

In this place James and I, and the man he loves, and X and all the unknown children between us will walk and talk and hold one another in comforting arms and rejoice in an eternity of presence. We will move through a white landscape as soft as feathers of snow. We will feel the lines drawn between us, violin strings, how each string has a sweet tension all its own, how it draws out from my heart like a bead of silver fire and plunges into yours, X, and vibrates with the feel of your soul, your kindness, your humor, your beauty; and from your heart to James, where the string resonates with all the love he holds, his passions and his fears, the desire of his hands to do good works; and from James into Brian, and from Brian to

The Lone and Dreary World

me, and from us into the never-ending, ever-changing, breaking crescendo of family, the family we are given and the family we choose, the souls we gather to our hearts, the strings we pluck, the harmonies we join. In the white land we all sing together. No one hurts anymore. No one cries anymore. Every note is heard. That's the way it will be, unending.

This is what you lose when you no longer believe in God.

9.

We were, we learned, in the tail end of Nebraska's storm season. I was used to regular summer storms but Rexburg's thunderheads were positively domestic by comparison with the fierce banks and shelves of cloud hanging over the wheat fields. They loomed, inverted step pyramids, banded like angry layer cakes, sculpted by a rotational wind that hinted at funnel clouds. Always the storms were accompanied by a dramatic light which stirred X. He loved the bright bruised sky against the luminous yellow of the fields, and whenever we noted a dark smudge on the horizon X became fidgety with anticipation.

One storm positioned itself obligingly just beyond a bizarre monument, old dead cars painted primer-gray and stacked and arranged to resemble Stonehenge. It was more than X could do to resist the scene. He tried to set up his easel but the nearness of the storm prevented it; he went chasing several pieces of watercolor paper across the weedy ground while the cloud cell turned lazily above the silent, brooding prairie. Some small bit of rubble picked up by the wind pinged against the hollow metal flank of an upturned Impala. The sound chilled me. We settled for photographs of the place.

Following X through the strange monument of Carhenge, I wondered what was here for him – here in me, in my presence. I was not so exciting as the cars or the blue storm-light. He hadn't drawn me again since that first time in his hotel room. My stomach knotted to realize that only now, when we had been gone from Rexburg for so long, had I even stopped to consider what X was getting out of our little adventure. Sex, certainly. Was that all I was to him, a mobile concubine? This is the kind of question normal women ask *before* they upturn their lives, I told myself. I had been so thrilled at the excuse to leave town that I had gone about it all slipshod and hasty, and now I was tied to a man for God knew what purpose.

The bank of cloud seemed to draw nearer. It certainly was taller and an alarming wash of indigo was now visible below it, the dragging stain of precipitation. That could be hail, X said. We'd better get going.

Carhenge disappeared behind the dust of our retreat. Only the storm could be seen through the hybrid's rear window, its forward face narrowing to a prominence that pointed in our direction with a long ominous finger of cloud. X squinted at it in his side mirror. "I'll get you, my pretty, and your little dog too."

Baptism for the Dead

"I need to ask you something," I said.

"Okay."

"Why are you with me?"

He laughed. "Why are you with me?"

"I mean, what are you getting out of this? I'm not so full of myself to think that I'm anything special. I'm not the most beautiful woman in the world. I'm not even single. I'm messed up and complicated. So why me? Why did you let me come with you?"

"You seemed like you needed a friend."

The roadside wheat bent before the wind. I watched it flatten and shake without answering. "Okay," X said. "There is a reason. I just don't know how to say it without sounding like a creep."

"Tell me. I need to know."

He pulled onto a side road that joined the highway at the site of a lone rusted mailbox affixed to a decrepit wooden stand. The road was only paved a few yards out; beyond, where it ran between barbed-wire fences and nominal pasture, it turned to dirt, and far out among the flat acreage the dark outline of an old house hunched in the wind. X watched me a moment, apprehensive. Then he tapped my elbow. I removed it from the glove box between us. It opened with a click. He sighed, and reached inside, and pulled out a small sketch pad with a brown cover and handed it to me. The sketch pad was old; its cover was stained and scored, the corners of its pages felted from years of handling. The spiral wire of its spine had relaxed at one end, unwinding itself through two or three perforations.

"Open it," X said.

I did. Inside it was full of faded drawings. Of me, I thought for a moment; but the more I looked at the woman on the pages the more subtle differences I saw between us. She was a few pounds heavier, more softly curved. Her naked breasts were slightly larger, her nose just barely more snubbed. Her hair was cut a bit shorter than I kept mine, but the similarities were astounding. We could have been sisters. We could have been twins.

"Who is this?" I looked up into X's face. He was frowning; he looked ashamed.

"Rebecca."

"Oh my God."

"I'm sorry. I should have told you. I was engaged to her once, but she left me. When I first saw you I couldn't believe how much you look like her. And at first it was almost the same, being with you. But now it's different.

Baptism for the Dead

Now that I know you, you're nothing like her, and I'm happy. I don't want her anymore."

But the sketch pad was right there in my hands, bearing testimony to X's lost love. "This is so strange," I said.

"I'm sorry."

"No. I have something to tell you, too." And I told him about Adam – everything, every memory I had of the boy, every memory I had of that summer. I was shaken to realize that telling it all took only minutes. Was it so small a thing, what had driven me all these years?

When I had spilled the entire story X shook his head. "We're a hell of a pair, aren't we?"

I paged through the sketch book again, staring at Rebecca as if I could memorize every small difference between her features and mine. X's ex. Were we real to each other at all, he and I? Or were we only proxies? A nauseating pressure was growing inside me, a certainty that what was once lost would never be regained. X and I were both chasing phantoms, running down fading tracks through the sagebrush. I remembered the day of my temple endowment, my wistful hope for some woman somewhere to wash me clean and set me free. I wondered how, by my mere presence, I was freeing X from the loss that haunted him, if I was freeing him at all.

The Lone and Dreary World

All at once the car vibrated, a tinny clatter. Outside hailstones bounced on the dirt road. The clatter rose to a roar.

"Hell," X said. The storm caught up to us. He reversed onto the empty highway and sped westward, trying to outrun the weather. I put the sketch pad back into the glove box. The hinge whispered. It sounded like a woman's sigh.

*

We did manage to outrun that storm. After ten silent minutes of driving the large, violent hail stones reduced in size and finally sputtered out altogether, and we drove fast toward a warm sunset. Neither of us spoke. The revelation of our dual proxyism left me feeling embarrassed, and although I couldn't say how X felt, he was chewing his lip and concentrating very hard on the road, his fingers tight and angular on the steering wheel.

Once the hail was well past us I felt compelled to break the silence.

"Well," I said. "I suppose this is a sign, isn't it?"

"A sign?"

"You look like my old boyfriend. I look like your old fiance. Don't you think this means something?"

X smiled. "It's quite a coincidence, I'll give you that."

"Really, though. This has to mean something."

We blew past a truck laden with hay bales. Bits of golden chaff twinkled in its wake and pattered against our windshield. X said nothing.

"You don't believe in signs?"

He shook his head. "Not really. But coincidences are amusing."

Amusing? The suggestion that I should find this amusing rubbed me the wrong way. I found it discomfiting that I should be the spitting image of Rebecca, that my resemblance to a lost partner should have been the thing that drew X to me. And I felt ashamed of that feeling, aware as I was that it was unfair to dislike X's motive when it was exactly the same as my own.

"Yeah," said X. "Don't you think this is kind of funny?"

I didn't know how to respond to that. I did feel like laughing, but there was such a flutter of hysteria in my chest that I didn't allow myself even to smile. "If you don't believe in signs, then what do you believe in?"

"You don't believe in signs, either."

"Of course I do."

"But you don't believe in God. Where do signs come from if they're not from God?"

He had me there. "Well, I don't know. The universe?"

"Want some ice cream?"

"Stop trying to change the subject." A little town gathered in clumps of dark trees off the highway. The stilt-legged signs of gas stations flickered alight, towering over homes built low against the Nebraska wind. It would soon be evening, warm and soft and wheat-scented. I thought of sitting on a sidewalk curb with Adam in the gathering night, drinking Slush Puppies so cold they hurt. "Yeah. Ice cream sounds good."

We parked on the edge of a deli's lot, where the pavement gave way to weeds. The crown of a pyramid of old tires peeked above the tops of waist-high grasses. The storm had turned and ran parallel to the highway now, a great body of purple cloud. We could smell it, a whiff of ice against the warmth of farmland. In a nearby field a flock of sheep bleated in fear and milled around a wooden shelter. The light was lowering. X bought ice cream bars and turkey sandwiches. We stood as we ate them, kicking at the fringe of weeds spilling onto the pavement.

I licked the last of the ice cream from my fingers. Food had steadied me. This was X, after all. Whatever his motives, he had been good to me. He was safe enough, I was sure of that.

"So tell me what you believe in," I said.

"I believe that this is the best turkey sandwich I've ever had."

I laughed. "Okay. And what else?"

"If you're asking what I think of God, he said, I'm an atheist."

That word felt terrible to me, hollow and cold, rattling like hailstones. I didn't know what to make of a person who used such a stark, bleak word to describe himself – his own self, living and warm and beautiful. He saw the look on my face.

"What are you worried about? You're an atheist, too."

"I am not!"

"You don't believe in God. You said so."

"I don't like that word."

The Lone and Dreary World

He put his arm around my shoulders. "It's just a word. I'm still me. You know me." "You have to believe in signs," I said. I was anxious to attach some significance to our relationship. If this all *meant* something, then it was all right that I'd left town with a virtual stranger, it was all right that I looked like the woman he had lost. It was all right that he labeled himself with that frightening word. It would all make sense in the end. "What am I if I'm not a sign?"

"You are more than a sign," he said. "You are you. I want you, not Rebecca." He kissed me. I kissed him back under the flickering light of the deli's sign, while the storm shouldered past us into the night.

The Nail in the Sure Place

The Nail in the Sure Place

1.

Almost two weeks after leaving Idaho we abandoned Nebraska and looped back into Wyoming. Between my fears over James and my discomfort with or respective proxyism, I had become a miserable traveling companion, too quiet and long-faced. And the gravity of belief had finally struck me with its full, open-eyed, gasping force. I had never considered what it meant to not believe in God. Preoccupied as I had been with blending in, with preserving the one life I knew how to live, I hadn't examined the consequences of non-belief. I had just *not believed*. Only when Brian had said his awful words to me did I realize that I no longer had any concept of James or me or anyone existing in an eternity of well-earned peace. There was no heaven, no judgment, no reward, nothing to make any of this worthwhile or all right in the end. There was no cosmic amelioration, no sense even to signs, no significance in Adam-X or ex-me. The fact of it rendered me blunt-edged and speechless.

X noticed the pall that had settled over me, of course. He was smarter than to tell me I shouldn't call James anymore. I really shouldn't have been calling James – not every day, at least – but the trauma I had inflicted on us was too spectacular. I couldn't make myself leave it

Baptism for the Dead

alone. I was compelled to talk to him as often as possible, to make sure he was still there, to do my miserable penance, and to spend the hours of driving in a fog of horrible pressing anxiety. It was stupid to call. I should have left him to Brian's care, to his own thoughts and the relief of my absence. I knew all this. X knew it, too. And he knew that what I needed was not a lecture or reassurance or quotes on the probability of follow-through on suicide threats. I needed a distraction. And so he took me to Cheyenne to show me a good time.

Now that I have visited far more interesting places, the idea of pursuing a good time in southeast Wyoming seems more than a little sad. But out in the wide-sky desolation of the prairies Cheyenne was our best option. It offered everything X needed to perk up my mood. Back then if you'd asked me how to show a friend a good time, I might have suggested home-baked cookies and a nice civil game of Uno. X had a more daring evening in mind.

"The first time I met you," he said, careful, testing, "you noticed I was drinking beer."

I waited. We had just dropped our travel bags onto a chair and luggage rack – a nicer hotel than we'd grown used to, with a luxury mattress, a flat-screen television inside a wooden hutch, and a halfdozen pillows on the extra-wide bed.

The Nail in the Sure Place

X went on cautiously, his voice belly-crawling, snake-low, "So how dead-set are you against alcohol?"

I thought for a moment, and then answered with a forced laugh that I'd left my husband and started an affair with a total stranger, some artist wandering through town. So I might as well go on as I'd started. "Oh, and there was caffeine in that iced tea you gave me the first night we met. I'm sure there was." My anxiety left in a welcome rush, and suddenly my laugh was real. The relief of honestto-God happiness made my skin prickle, it was so foreign. Had it been so long since I'd had fun? And really, what would it hurt after all? For God's sake, I'd broken every rule *but* the one about alcohol, and X was standing with his hands in his pockets, grinning his big broad-mouthed grin. I was worn down and hollowed out. Something momentous and new felt like just the thing to scrub the memory of Brian's phone call from my mind. I wanted something to make me believe I had never heard those words. I was ready to try anything.

"I'll take you out to a real cowboy bar," X said.

"If I puke you have to clean it up."

"I guarantee you that won't happen. I'll cut you off before you disgrace yourself."

Baptism for the Dead

I made myself as presentable as I could with what I had in my travel bags, fixing my hair with a focus that kept me from examining too closely the knot of nerves in my stomach. Alcohol was an absolute no-no back in town – back in the Church. But I was ready to give pious Rexburg a sock in the jaw. I couldn't think of a better place to stage a rebellion than a cowboy bar. I fussed over my hair and watched in the mirror as X got rid of his travel-worn t-shirt in that particular way he had, crossed arms, ducked head, glasses still on, pulling on a sleeveless white undershirt that made him look somehow thinner and more wiry, yet stronger – a dun musky animal – intensely desirable, more impossible to resist than ever before. Was I allowing him to take me someplace I was not ready to go, and only because he was so fascinating? Probable answers to that question made me embarrassed for myself, so I preferred not to think about it. I had called up the troops. I was committed to the rebellion. X led the charge.

"Giddyup," he said, that voice like a rip in velvet.

The moment we set foot outside the lobby of our fancy hotel all my effort in front of the mirror was wasted. Cheyenne's most outstanding feature is its wind. It pulled my hair from its bobby pins with a whack to my face and a roar in my ears. Ha, I said, shaking

The Nail in the Sure Place

my head until my hair was as wild and tangled as sage brush. X smiled.

Even with the constant breeze, even though the sun had almost set, the evening was still warm, and downtown Cheyenne graded around the edges toward a violet dusk. The oncoming darkness was deep-water blue. The wind kicked a torn brightly-colored bit of newspaper down the sidewalk, and X followed it past traffic lights and mats of littered ground cover flanking empty parking lots. Slinking between purple shadows, he chased some dark instinct that led him directly to a source of alcohol. Dangerous X with his lanky arms and his sharp nose in silhouette against the sky. X with his hidden history, X who didn't believe in signs but followed them all the same. I watched him from the corner of my eye, half afraid but excited, keeping pace with his easy gait as if this were nothing at all, as if I was accustomed to going out drinking every night. If I allowed myself to think too hard about whether I really wanted to do this, I might call the whole thing off – the bar and Cheyenne, the road trip and X and Adam and all.

We passed a Dairy Queen, brightly lit. There was an old pickup truck in the lot, shining on one side with the artificial crimson glow of the shop's sign. A group of teenage boys rough-housed in the truck bed. They were all barked shouts and neon luminosity, tense with a tight feral energy I had never seen in boys before. The righteous sons of Rexburg do not wrestle in parking lots on windy nights. X grinned at the boys; his eye teeth glimmered. There was a hint of the same wildness in him tonight. Was it the wind that sharpened him, or the prospect of a little fun? Or did that blue prairie gale sharpen me, blow the dust from my eyes so that now I saw X more clearly, a lean hunting cat of a man who could wait in unsuspecting dull Rexburg until his prey stumbled by? The incident with the secret sketch pad proved how little I knew him, what a fool I had been to leave with him. He seemed menacing and strange, and yet I was not frightened. I wanted him more, and the escape he promised, the distraction.

Before long he found what he was looking for: a wood-fronted bar called the Crooked Leg. Its single dark window like a punched eye looked out at us, squinted at us where we stood on the sidewalk.

"You ready?" X said. His hair moved constantly in the wind, a dark tangle. He was savage and compelling. In answer I pushed open the door myself and led him inside.

*

The Nail in the Sure Place

There was a tavern in Rexburg. Just one. It was stuck self-consciously beside a tax accountant's office in a dingy half-dead strip mall out on the edge of town. No one ever recognized the few cars parked outside. Whoever ran the tavern and whoever frequented it must have been strangers to Rexburg – the blur on the social periphery, Catholic immigrant farm workers, stranded businessmen, wayward depressives. Whenever we passed it on our shopping outings my girlfriends would roll their eyes or tut in disapproval and the car would fill with a momentary sensation of wariness. Drinkers were dangerous. Everybody knew that.

I couldn't help thinking about the tavern-goers, who they were, what they did inside. Drink, of course – but was there some fellowship behind its painted glass door that I deserved to be a part of, some secret handshake of the nonbelievers which I needed to learn? I was often tempted to slip inside. What deterred me was the ever-present police car in the strip mall's parking lot. The professor's wife could not be seen in a place like that, surrounded by drunks, giving the Sure Sign of the Apostate, the raised glass clinking.

Sometimes I imagined the tavern in Rexburg concealed some kind of dark dread, that its

Baptism for the Dead

dense atmosphere of bleakness might suck me in if I gave into temptation and wandered too near, a black hole capturing Jesus's sunbeam. In that sense it had the same gravitational pull on me as Adam had, although for James's sake I never got close enough to the tavern to allow its claws into my skin. Still, I would spend some lonely Thursday and Friday nights parked in my car across the highway from that strip mall, watching the despondent flybuzz shiver of the bar's lit red sign on the verge of burnout. I never recognized the people who came and went. There weren't many of them. They were nobodies.

*

The Crooked Leg was nothing like I'd thought Rexburg's solitary bar to be. It looked quietly menacing from the street, but once we were inside my anxiety began to abate. Slowly. My heart no longer raced, but my senses were still on high alert. I was a small frail animal emerging from its burrow. There was a good-sized crowd here, all of them smiling. The place was dim and the room decidedly dark-colored, old wood paneling and sepia light, but the prevailing mood was not one of despair. You can loosen up, I told myself sensibly.

The Nail in the Sure Place

Everybody is having a good time. Country music jangled like my tender nerves, just loud enough that X had to lean toward my ear to be heard: "I'll order something for you." And his voice undercut the cacophony with a force that made me hold my breath as I nodded my head, mute and helpless.

He sat me down at the low table for two against a dark wall and excused himself to the bar. Pictures of old Cheyenne tilted a little in their frames. A girl wearing a black half-apron, with a heart tattooed on her wrist, deposited a wooden bowl of pretzels on my table. I ate so many, just for something to do, that by the time X returned with two glasses of beer my mouth was uncomfortably, almost painfully, dry.

"Pale ale," he announced.

The glass bumped down in front of me. It sweated a little, twinkling dully in the subdued brown light. I sweated a little.

X raised his glass toward me. "Cheers," he said.

I knew from movies and from some dim instinct of social convention that I was expected to respond in kind. The glass was heavier than it should have been. When I lifted it a little beer spilled over the rim and onto my cold wet fingers. Our glasses clanked together. I returned mine to the tabletop and licked my knuckles; the flavor was earthy and overwhelmingly bitter, not at all pleasant, and my agitated imagination drew up my first taste of beer as a rough sketch of me standing in the middle of a beautiful sunlit wheat field, being punched in the stomach by an unseen fist.

X saw the look on my face. "It's an acquired taste."

"Then why does anybody drink it?"

"You acquire the taste quickly. Have a sip."

"I don't know about this."

"Everything that's good should taste a little bad at first, don't you think?"

"No, I do not think, and that sounds like an awful cliché besides." But he had a point. X was the only thing keeping me sane and distracted while I pulled further and further from Rexburg, stretching whatever tethered me there until it was thin enough to snap. And he tasted bitter now, with his sketch pads hidden in secret compartments, with his penchant for proxies.

I sipped my beer. I felt the sharp impact of the bitterness on my tongue and in my gut. I kept my eyes on X, who watched me soberly as I drank swallow after swallow. And soon the taste in my mouth was not bitter, but golden and homey and soft, bread baking, chewing raw kernels of wheat in the summer sun. The memory of X drawing in his hotel room came back to me powerfully, the sketch pad resting on his knee, the easy unfocusing of my eyes, the smell of linseed oil warming between us.

"It is good," I said, surprised.

"I think she's acquired a taste."

As the night grew later, the Crooked Leg drew a larger crowd. We had found the center of Cheyenne nightlife, such as it was. A DJ appeared, unshaven and tattooed; between requested country hits he encouraged patrons to ride the mechanical bull, an ugly hunk of hide and machinery tilted up at a hysterical angle under a halo of colored lights, surrounded by a padded floor.

"Ride the bull, X!" X declined.

I had reached the bottom of my second beer. My limbs felt loose, alive with vibration. "It's either the bull or me."

"Good God! What a mouth. You're cut off."

"Am I drunk?" I asked him, trying to process the prickling in my arms, which were, unaccountably, resting still on the table beside my empty glass and not floating as I had initially thought.

Baptism for the Dead

"Not very," he said, "but drunk enough." He paid the tab. "Let's blow this popsicle stand. You ought to get some fresh air, lightweight."

By now the bar was rowdy around the seams. Men in Stetsons laughed a little too loud, hunched a little too close over their drinks. Women moved too loosely. Their skirts were very short, and I was slightly dizzy; my mind crept along uncertainly after my body. X put his arm around me, guided me out into the windy night.

In Cheyenne we bayed like dogs at blinking traffic lights. We did cartwheels in an abandoned, silent park. X collided with the dark form of two statue boys, frozen in a run, invisible in the darkness. I climbed onto the back of one and rode him like a racehorse, whooping, then shrieked when I realized I couldnt get down again. X pressed against me and I slithered back to earth, my face and chest against the cold metal, my back hot against his skin. When we had run enough that our legs began to shake we climbed onto the stage of a great wooden amphitheater and watched the flicker of distant headlights through a line of windbreak trees, trucks passing on the Interstate.

I felt loosened and calm enough to ask the question that had haunted me since I had talked to Brian in Nebraska. I was able at last,

The Nail in the Sure Place

in fact, to frame the question in words – to understand the dragging weight of dread and bleakness in my gut, and to name it.

"So if there is no God, then what do we believe happens after we die?"

"We?"

"People who don't believe."

"I'm not a physicist," X said carefully. "And I've had a few beers. I'm just an artist. But there's this principle in science, a way nature works. Matter and energy can't be destroyed. Can't be made, either. It's all here from the beginning, taking different forms."

"Reincarnation?"

"I don't think so. Not the way most people think of it. Everything that has form..." he kissed my neck "...came from some other form that fell apart."

"Where is this going?"

"I said I'm not a physicist. When you die, you die, and that's it."

"That's terrible." Unthinkable. I had been raised my whole life to expect the white place, the Veil, the faces and hands, eternity. "That's it? You die? You fall apart?"

X read the tension in my body. "What's so

bad about that? I think it's poetic."

"It's depressing." Desolation and nothingness.

"Was it depressing before you were born? It's the same."

"All right. So things fall apart, and after you die, you're nowhere."

"Don't sound so sad. Look. When you die, you fall apart, you revert to all the little bits that make up you, all the atoms. And those atoms are re-used by nature, and they make something else. Everything else. Animals and trees and storms. You transform."

"And your thoughts? Your consciousness? Your mind?"

"Energy. All that's nothing but energy, the action of your brain cells. The energy that was you goes out into the world and becomes wind, and lightning."

"That is not poetic, X."

"I'm not a poet, either. This is the way I look at it: if there is nothing after I die, then every second of life I have means so much more. I've got to fit it all in now. And I've got to appreciate it, because it's not permanent. When I'm gone, I'm gone."

"You find that comforting?"

The Nail in the Sure Place

"I find it horrible, and beautiful, and true."

I stared at the distant illuminated line of the Interstate. The flicker of headlights scored bright lines into my vision. I saw them when I closed my eyes and leaned my head on X's shoulder, a vivid echo of movement, lines crossing lines innumerable as stars, as bright and inviting as neon across a highway.

2.

Interstate 80 rescued us from the plainness of the Plains, restoring us to a familiar mountain landscape. To the west the horizon broke in a blue haze, and the haze solidified into mountain peaks as even as spread fingers, and before too many more miles the foothills of the Wyoming Range resolved out of a distant dust of antelope herds and truckers' convoys. By afternoon we were on the downward slope of a narrow mountain pass, switching back, descending into a canyon where, in the heat of the brief Rocky Mountain summer, cottonwoods were beginning to yellow in patches of blurred-leaf motion. When the highway leveled out we sped long the banks of a stream, rapid and pencil-blue, smelling cold as under-ripe apples through the car's air vents.

Suburban Utah greeted us with a wide sweep of road, white slashes of church steeples blinking at regular intervals along distant hills. Being among the civilized again made me feel ponderous with guilt. All the houses we passed, built in proximity to good schools and shopping centers, were a tally of my failures as a Mormon, as a wife, as a woman. The satellite towns circling the orbit of Salt Lake brimmed with happy families, kids playing with dogs in yards, wives cooking supper for husbands stuck in traffic. This was a population of men and women who had faced down their personal adversities and had made it all work – something James and I had failed to do. This was a population that knew the white place was real, that would not fall apart after death and dissipate in a sparkling shower of atoms. As I held X's hand on the glove box between our seats I cringed inside with the force of my shame and fear. I loved the hand I held, I loved X's smile, his laugh, everything. But I had taken James as my husband, and I owed my allegiance to him. Only by returning to our life together could I set my wrongs to right.

And only by returning could I shake off the torment of X's afterlife. He called it beautiful, but I could not discern any beauty in falling apart. Maybe I didn't believe in God, but in Rexburg I could perhaps soothe my fear of an eternity of disintegration. Surrounding myself with people who believed in the Celestial Kingdom might somehow make that part of religion, at the very least, real.

These were my only clear thoughts as we had our early dinner on the second-story patio of a restaurant in Salt Lake City's red brick shopping square. I floated somewhere above the conversation, though I let X think I was as engaged as ever, as with him as ever. But all the while I was thinking I ought to run back home and beg James to forgive me, and we would go on once more as if none of this had ever happened, until we died and went to Heaven, which had to exist. It just had to.

Two women sitting at a nearby table complained delicately over their salads. I tuned in to their conversation through the static fuzz inside my head. "I couldn't bring Madison with me because they don't let kids under five on the patio anymore. Some baby got its head stuck in the railing and now there's liability issues."

Perhaps I ought to stick my head through the railing, I thought. The change of perspective might do me some good. By the time X has figures out how to unstick me I'll have come to a decision.

Sunset was approaching, and X, who had never seen Salt Lake before, wanted to explore before it got too dark. We paid our tab and I led him toward the heart of downtown, the castle spire of the courthouse with its white clock face mimicking the pale heads of the Wasatch peaks behind. Beyond, the triplicate towers of the Salt Lake Temple soared into a flawless blue sky, the statue of golden Moroni poised with raised trumpet above the precision grid of the city's streets.

"I've got to see that up close," X said, emphatic, staring at the temple.

The Nail in the Sure Place

I figured the very heart of Mormonism was the most poetically satisfying place to end my all-too-brief freedom. *This is the place*, as they say.

I agreed.

Since finishing dinner I could not seem to get the image of the dog in Driggs out of my mind, brittle bleached fur, twist of twine. My decision had been made for me. *Foreordained*, Moroni whispered from his perch.

We made our way past dress shops and spaces for lease in the old quarter, past a gay bar where a handsome man was setting tall tables and bar stools outside the old stone building. Its pale blocks were set firm and straight by good Mormon masons in the days of Brigham Young, the founding days, and now it was a place for men to meet men. What irony, you Saints. While X chattered happily about something – some art technique, some school of thought – I nodded automatically and watched the bartender bend over his work. There were lean long muscles in his arms. He caught my eye and smiled, friendly. I smiled back, resigned. I wondered whether James would find this man attractive. When I came home. When I picked up and dusted off the good life from where I had dropped it. Moroni's trumpet was tootling in my ear, a victory march that drowned out the sweet soft music of X's voice.

Baptism for the Dead

I don't believe in fore-ordainment, I told myself and Moroni firmly. My thoughts sounded very small and frail against the squawk of his horn.

We arrived in Temple Square just as the sky began to burn orange. Lights came on around the grounds and atop the temple walls, floods pointing upward to bathe the angular layers of steeple on steeple with an ascendant white glow, a light that seemed to stretch the very architecture, the bone of stone and steel, up toward heaven.

X removed a small sketch pad from his back pocket and frantically, rapturously drew the great elongated lines of the temple, its overhead lean, its custodial glower. I kept my eyes on his hands, his lovely long hands, how they moved over the paper, the sound the skin of his knuckle made as it dragged softly across the surface. Oh God, I would miss his hands, and this was how I would always remember them, delineating the bars of my prison.

X handed me his camera and posed between the immoveable bronze statues of Joseph and Hyrum Smith, who gazed steadfast and unseeing into a distance of city blocks while X pointed both his forefingers like guns at the camera, at me, and winked. I thought, I must remember to ask him for that picture later. It will be nice to keep, so I can remember his smile, too.

"I want to come back here and paint it in the morning," X said.

I just wanted to get away from the place. It was taunting me and my pathetic spring for freedom. Many are the plans in a man's heart, but it is the Lord's purpose that prevails... or something to that effect. Proverbs? Word of Wisdom? I should know this. A good Mormon would know. But in spite of my readiness to surrender and retreat, the prospect of one more night in one more hotel room skin to skin with X was a stronger lure than I could resist. And what was the harm? The Greyhound station would still be waiting for me in the morning; the price of a ticket back to Rexburg would not have changed over the course of a single night. I would set him free then to find Rebecca, to chase that wisp of a ghost out across the West.

And I still hadn't asked him for that picture.

One last night.

Baptism for the Dead

3.

I made our final night last as long as I could. The hotel was not quiet. Somewhere on the same block loud music played, an aggressive beat upside-down over the muted tin fuzz of blown-out speakers. Occasionally voices would raise in brief shouting matches or a bottle would break against the black pavement with a small hollow burst like a Christmas light dropped on a floor. So we couldn't fall asleep anyhow. And even after the police arrived to restore some semblance of propriety, hours after dark, I kept X going, so that at first he laughed in disbelief at my appetite, and then he begged some time to recover, and finally he fell asleep altogether, murmuring something that was half apology, half protest, while his fingers, at least, tried to stay awake for a minute or two more.

His hand twitched lightly where it lay against my thigh. His breath was deep. It sighed over his parted lips. A police car drove a warning circuit around the block; through the crack in the heavy dullcolored curtains of our room the patrol car's lights flashed red-blue, red-blue; the light flickered across X's face, over his exposed teeth, the slope of his shoulder. Then the car was gone, and the room lapsed once more into near-darkness. From somewhere – the street

The Nail in the Sure Place

lamp? – a wan, gray light illuminated the fine hairs of X's body, so the line of his arm and side, even the folded edge of his ear, stood out just barely from the night. I wondered if he dreamed of Rebecca. I wondered if he would try to stop me tomorrow when I insisted that he take me to the bus station. I wondered if his dreams, like his memories, would become someday a wind storm, lightning. Particles of me, my energy, the electricity of X's nerves, flashing in the sky before it rips and groans with thunder.

I don't remember ever approaching sleep that night, but I woke, the sheets tangled around my legs, the blanket gone altogether (found, after a moment, on the floor on X's side of the bed). A thin bar of intense yellow sunlight split the curtains. I squinted at it. I had jolted awake on some memory, some old lesson, and now I struggled to catch whatever stray image had roused me and examine it, a pale moth in a dirty jar. Dogged, it evaded me. I retraced my first strange thoughts back through waking into whatever dream-state I had been in, a realm between sleep and sorrow. I saw the ghosts of men standing on great white blocks, scaffolding, blurred old photographs – a Sunday school project, a trip to the Rexburg library. Dimly I recalled writing notes on the construction of the Salt Lake Temple. I must have been twelve years old then. While

Baptism for the Dead

I worked I had chewed an enormous wad of grape bubblegum, secretly and slowly, because gum was not allowed in the library. Facing X's naked back, the remembered taste of the gum suddenly filled my mouth. I swallowed a mouthful of saliva.

It had taken forty years to build the temple. Forty years of labor, part of it during a war with the United States, who had not wanted to yield Mormon country to the Mormons. All that work, all that danger – for what? For a building. A pretty one yes; sublime, even, but can't a religion survive without a forty-year construction project? Can't an almighty God dwell wherever the hell he likes?

Grape bubblegum. A spiral notebook with a pink cover, filled with my childish handwriting, all curlicues and great round circles to dot the Is. Jesus wants me for a sunbeam. All that fuss over a building. All that fuss over cathedrals in Europe, pyramids in Egypt. All the fuss X makes when he draws and redraws until he gets the lines just right, the shape just right, the expression on my face just right when I take off my garments and lay them on a chair in a hotel in Rexburg, a world away. There is a cave in Southern France where, thirty-eight thousand years ago, ancient men drew by torchlight the images of animals in motion. There is a rhinoceros drawn and redrawn so that its horn rises just so from the face; behind

The Nail in the Sure Place

the stark lines of the animal's shape you can see the erasures where some long-dead man wearing only furs fussed and played until his painting looked just right. The voice of my art appreciation professor rose up in my mind like a vapor: *Van Gogh once said, The world is a study of God which has turned out badly.* We are all trying so hard to get something just right; even God, if you would believe Van Gogh, and for my part, I believe him more than I believe any prophet.

What drives us to press on for forty years, or a hundred, or a thousand, to create something so precise and true? What is the magic spell in the act of creation? I felt the answer was just at my fingertips where they rested tingling a millimeter from X's skin. I touched him lightly. I ran my fingers up the length of his spine to his hairline. This was a new circuit beneath his skin, a new faint memory that would fall apart one day. He held his breath in his sleep for what seemed an eternity. Then he resumed, sleep hardly interrupted, breath audible and animal, and I stopped breathing instead for as long as I could, until my lungs and throat burned.

4.

X found a likely spot and set up his easel, tied on his green half-apron with its burden of brushes and rags. I spread a blanket on a well-tended lawn beneath a mother and her children, petrified in bronze, dancing below the temple spires. We were surrounded by the most riotous, transient colors, X and the statue family and I: pansies and mums just getting started, intense deep violet and orange; creeping ground cover with tiny stars of white and pink; coleus with leaves like shreds of citrus peel, tart in the sun. The spring planting of tulips had mostly been excised by the Temple groundskeepers, but here and there a missed stalk stood above its quivering blade leaves, a few pale petals drooping from the white ring below the lone pistil and the ragged, spent anthers. The crush of color was intimidating. So much life here, so may bees rising and settling amid the garden beds, so many birds dashing across the grass just out of reach of the people wandering the paths in their smart Sunday clothes (though it was, in fact, Tuesday). There was a frantic feel to the garden. After a moment I realized why: most of these flowers were annuals. The tulips would sleep beneath the snow, but the rest would sigh and give up and wilt in the fall, and gardeners would dig

The Nail in the Sure Place

them up and replace them next spring with more of their kind. In the meantime they did what they could to make their mark and make their seeds, to progress into their own small eternity. The great disordered shout of color wound all around the statue, Bronze Mom and Bronze Brood, dull even in the sunshine, halted mid-whirl, statuestill, while every petal of every blossom vibrated with life and with the breeze. Ring around the rosie, we all fall down – except if we're made of bronze. Then we may be eternally perfect, sure enough, but we've got to watch the flowers try and die every year, year after year.

In a mood like this it was a good thing I stayed far from X. God knows how his painting might have turned out otherwise. Little black rainclouds hanging over the temple.

Before we returned to Temple Square I made a stack of sandwiches: white bread, peanut butter and jelly, all put back into the bread bag and secured with a knot to keep ants away. When I reached into the bag to pull one out a smear of peanut butter tracked along the back of my hand. I licked my hand clean and watched X at his easel. From this angle I couldn't see what he painted, but I could see the jump of a muscle in his arm as he made a repeated, rapid dart at his watercolor paper, tap tap tap. I had the feeling of lifting, drifting, bisecting into two people as I chewed my

Baptism for the Dead

sandwich. Rebecca used to watch him paint, surely. How could she not? X would not miss me when I got on the bus. I was a standin, Rebecca the Sequel. And he was not X but Adam, and Adam was gone, would never come again. What a destructive, idiot fool I had been.

People stopped. I learned over the course of our brief travels that nothing draws gawkers like X's easel. An artist at work is a summoning bell. Hikers and travelers, sight-seers and true believers all dipped and fell into his lone orbit, circled him casually, passed behind his back and glanced over his shoulder before wandering on a few steps, turning as if a thought had just occurred to them, returning to stand still just at the edge of his vision. Once they were rooted in place he always smiled slightly and nodded, then returned to his paper and brushes. His watchers stood rapt for minutes at a time, then drifted away with an air of having been graced – calmed, enlightened, connected somehow to the artist though X had done nothing more than acknowledge them in a friendly, if distracted, way. Sometimes the watchers struck up conversation. X engaged peripherally – friendly still, but focused on his work. They wanted to tell him stories. "My aunt paints," they'd say, eager to share something with X, eager to know that he and they were of a kind.

To witness an act of creation rouses a primal kinship. Who has not felt the desire to stand against a cool cave wall and press to its face a hand red with ocher, red with heart's blood? My palm tingles for want of stone beneath it. Who has not wanted to make and to tell the world, I *made* this – *I* made this – this is what I saw, this is what I know; this is the hasty moment of a single life, a moment I chose above all others to exalt, to show you, whoever you are; to carry on for me when I am nothing, not even a name – but this is what I knew, and this is what I made.

*

My aunt paints. X was sweet as could be to the people who stopped to engage him but when we were alone he often rolled his eyes over the things they would say. "Your aunt," he said to me, addressing his long-gone admirers, "paints crap." Your aunt paints nauseating cabin scenes without any sense of distance or atmosphere. Your aunt paints miserable still-lifes with the vase of flowers smack in the center of the canvas, with straight white paint for the petals, no tint of color, no understanding of how light works, how colorful white is, how the colors fool the eye into seeing white amid a garish pale rainbow of reflections. No understanding of the delicate

Baptism for the Dead

coolness of violet shadow beneath leaves. X studied this stuff with the fervor of a priest. X felt the throb of light and shade as a sob of worship in his throat. He licked the bristles of his brushes to keep them well shaped, and the taste of them on his tongue was as holy as sacrament bread.

I understood his outrage. Couldn't these passers-by see that he was more than a casual hobbyist? Didn't his discipline show? If he could make no better impression on the world than to summon images of Aunt Matilda and her rancid chalk-white still-lifes, then what was all this work and worship for?

But I was more forgiving of the painting aunts. They were casual, perhaps even silly in their understanding of beauty, and their attempts to render it were novice and unaware. But their devotion was not insincere, and their need to make and to pass along their making was as real and as urgent as any master's.

One day, somewhere between Chimney Rock and the Wyoming border, along a stretch of highway flanked on one side by twelve oxen in scenic pasture, the figure of an old man at a French easel dissolved in reverse through the road dust and the dimness of distance. He stood knee-deep in weeds across a wide ditch slashed with the shoots of wild asparagus. His arms were browned from years of painting

The Nail in the Sure Place

in the sun. An old fedora obscured his eyes. X pressed the button to lower the passenger window. "My aunt paints!" he yelled as we sped past. The man did not look up from his easel. I imagined that he heard in X's shout some acknowledgment of kinship, the artist's handshake. Or perhaps he heard nothing above the vibration of the road.

In any case, he went on painting.

*

A cluster of tourists gathered near X, but instead of the usual scene of quiet satisfaction an air of disbelief fairly crackled around his easel. A middle-aged woman and man leaned their heads together to whisper. The woman's hand moved up and down in an emphatic gesture. A young mother took two of her children by the hands and hauled them away. A third boy trailed after her, turning as he walked to shuffle backward, to take in a final look at the man painting in Temple Square. On other faces I saw tense lips, frowns, glances side-eye. I stood, stretched the tension from my legs, and approached the crowd, quietly, hands in pockets, blending in.

"...not very respectful, that's all I'm

Baptism for the Dead

saying." Tail end of the whispering woman's conversation.

From the edge of the crowd I found a clear view of X's easel, and what I saw transfixed me. It is hard to explain why. It was, after all, merely a painting of the temple. But it was not. Though the structure itself was recognizable, the edges were blurred, great clouds of pigment and water bleeding across the page, bleeding into the sky. Where the hard-line edge of stone wall should have been, the paint fanned in tendrils fine as feather-fur, fingers spread and desperate against the gaudy pale colors of a white that was not white. The more I stared at the paper the more I saw how wrong it was. The walls were too tall, the garden below too flat and dull. Crenelations as sharp as smiles tore at too-bright sky. The steeples leaned toward one another as if to repudiate absolutely the watchers at X's easel, even the painter himself; and above them an angular dark slash hung suspended in blue, Moroni dispossessed of his spire or a blind bird in flight.

X raised a brush and laid it against the paper. The surface lifted minutely in response to his touch, gleamed wet and eager; for a heartbeat nothing happened, and the crowd could not look away for the awfulness of waiting. Then a bead of blue dropped from the bristles, ran down the wall of the temple, streaking it, a long hot track of sharp sky weeping onto the

The Nail in the Sure Place

stern, garish stone, trailing all the way to the earth.

Shrugs in the crowd. Heads shaking, confusion and even sadness written plain on faces. It was not that X had painted a terrible portrait of the temple. He was no Aunt Matilda. The image was strange and unlovely, but his skill was evident – the paint had gone where he'd willed it, done just what he commanded. And that was the point. He had made the temple into something the tourists did not recognize, or something they recognized too well – something bent and flawed, something indistinct, something that could be turned by any hand into any shape desired; something that could be rendered and obscured; something that was, ultimately, no more firm than water. X had not put a single mark wrong; this distortion was deliberate, and its frankness offended.

One young man with a trim haircut and a clean shave, smiling, tried to dispel the crowd's tension with humor. He said to X, "I don't know, man. I don't see it." A few grateful chuckles. X grinned. He did not look up from his painting.

"I think it's pretty." This came from a girl standing near her mother. I had not noticed her until she spoke. She had glossy brown hair pulled back with a headband that sparkled in the sun. Her eyebrows were thick and dark, but they did not look out of place on her sharp-boned face. She was perhaps just old enough to know what is truly pretty and what is not, and not yet old enough to do anything about it. Her arms folded below her small breasts. When she spoke, her mother turned red and clicked her tongue in disapproval, but the girl ignored the mother.

My eyes lifted from the painting to the temple beyond it, and in the warmth of the sun I allowed my eyes to lose focus. I squinted; the walls darkened and stretched, blurred around the edges. The surety of stone dissipated. There was no stone at all, only white light in a blue sky, only a pillar of cloud that might have blown away on any chance wind. I squinted harder, until my eyelids trembled, and stoic Moroni lifted from his spire and floated into the air, broke into a ragged shape, a reflection of leaves in water. When my eyes closed the dark side of my eyelids glowed with golden light. I said to myself, It's pretty.

I was not going to the bus station. Not today or any day.

5.

So X is an artist, a sly changer of forms, a transmogrifier of temples. That's where he fits into the world. He and the man on the side of the road with the easel and the fedora, he and all the painting aunts.

Where did I fit? What was my place in...not in Creation, but in this world of systems and order, of habitats and towns, a world where things fall apart in the end? I was not Rebecca; that much I did know. I had no idea whether X knew it.

In Rexburg everybody had a place. Everybody had a goal. The goal was the same: attain exaltation: the best afterlife, the White Land in perpetuity. As a woman I would be a wife and a mother and I would raise my children to achieve this goal. But now such a vastness of possibility opened up before me that I was immobilized by variety. Potential futures spread out before me like nets of nerves, each one electrified and tingling.

We stopped to gas up. I got out of the car and stretched, cracked my spine, sighed with relief. I had been feeling a pinch in my belly all day, and I realized that my period had at last come. Not going to be a mother – not yet, anyway, thank God. I knew I had packed some pads down in the bottom of the old green duffel bag I'd had since I was a kid. While X filled the tank, squinting in the heat, I dug underneath my clothes, rumpling them, searching by feel. My fingers found something hard and small and cold.

I drew it out, held it up to the sun. It hadn't seen it since my slumber party days. It was a small silvery ring, scratched and dulled with years, plain band bearing a little badge like the one on Superman's chest, but green, and instead of an S, these letters in a bold, heroic font: CTR.

We all had these. I was given mine at girls' camp, in a campfire ceremony with marshmallows and songs, surrounded by my fellow Beehive girls, our knees and faces gawkish in the firelight. The Laurel girls – the girls in high school, long-haired and beautiful and ripe with a feeling of expected adventure (graduation, marriage) – passed the rings out in a hushed atmosphere of belonging. Now we were part of the group. Now we were really Young Women. I recall slipping my ring onto a finger and staring at those letters. CTR. I would always have the ring to remind me, one of the Laurels intoned, when I was faced with a difficult decision. The ring was all the wisdom I needed.

Choose The Right.

The Nail in the Sure Place

I slid the ring onto my finger now, in the station lot sharp with the scent of spilled gasoline. How strange that I should find the ring again, at the moment when I was faced with every possible decision, with an avalanche of possibility, at a moment when the whole world was branching and rebranching, a road map endlessly unfolding.

"Well?" I asked the ring.

But Choose The Right was the best advice my past could offer me, and that, as it turned out, was no help at all.

6.

Early in the morning the causeway was abandoned. An endless bar of cloud above the Wasatch range trapped the dawn light, threw it back onto the surface of the Great Salt Lake where it glimmered below a reflection of mountains, bright lavender. Space was reversed. There was more water than sky. The mountains were the bruised tips of little fingers, the water too close for comfort. Along the causeway's narrow rocky shoulders the occasional skinny stand of sage broke the gravel. Above each brush a ripple in the air like a heat shimmer moved. As we drew closer and passed, the mirages revealed themselves as colonies of gnats spinning over the shrubs, voracious blue cyclones. Horned grebes ducked underwater. The dense surface of the lake stilled almost immediately; the grebes resurfaced in my side-view mirror as specks, corks bobbing. The peak of Antelope Island rose in front of us, growing taller and sharper and more varied in color, its featureless dun becoming a multiplicity of patches and striations, ochers, olive-greens, golds, a somber warm umber crown at its ancient apex.

We reached the island and, in reverence, drove along its eastern side. From this distance the gray suburbs of Salt Lake City lay motionless.

The Nail in the Sure Place

Far below the roadway the mountains side dropped to a ragged plain incised by a heavy streak of stunted dark trees and the finer, broken line of an old wire fence, its posts leaning into the grasses. Beyond, long-dried shoreline gave way to the pale wrack of salt flat, shot through with delicate silver cracks, and further still, a breadth of lake water hung heavy with reflected mountains.

Around a bend in the hill's side X braked hard. A sudden herd of bison drifted like continents from one side of the road to the other. They were as dark as basalt and as immoveable. We both sensed this, and made no attempt to hurry them. I held tight to X's hand as, one after another, they passed before us, feet from our bumper, processional, magnificent. One rolled its eye to meet my own – it was as small and gleaming as a ring, rimmed in damp white and red, adorned by a single large diamondwinged fly at its stone-black canthus. Over the quiet whirr of our engine we heard the bison's breath like a bellows. A foreleg connected to the earth, the fat and muscle along the long, tall shoulder rippled for an instant, and I could swear I felt the vibration of the heavy cloven footstep. Shed hair peeled in swathes from the muscular back. And then the last of them was gone, comically small rump following great head and shoulders over the verge of the road, down the hill to better grazing below, where the breeze would lift off the flies and scatter them away.

We moved on.

Larks called from the dry slopes beside the road. X stopped the car. A thin trail of packed dust the color of bone ran up the hillside between clumps of mullein. We took that trail. The larks perched atop the mullein stalks; they swayed in the slight breeze; they took turns shouting their proclamations. The island's flank stirred and sighed with the sound of wind. Upslope, a tiny long-legged owl skittered onto the trail, stopped to examine us, stretched one leg and one wing together in a display of nonchalance, then disappeared into the brush. When we reached the place where he had paused I saw how his little scribe-talons had scratched indiscernible hieroglyphs into the dust of the trail.

We climbed for a good twenty minutes or more. The trail led us to a pile of decaying boulders at the crest of a hill, dark with grains of lichen. X and I clambered atop them. Just as he pulled me to my feet to stand beside him a commotion erupted on the far side of the boulders, a loud rattle of pebbles, a crack and pop of stone on stone, and the receding heartbeat of hooves against earth. A tawny blur veered past us, white-orange-black. Before we could even jump in fright the pronghorn was gone, bolting down the hill beside the trail. X laughed, put his arm around me, warm. He smelled of dust and sweat and larks in the sun.

"Poor guy," he said. "We ruined his hiding spot."

Near our car the pronghorn slowed to a dignified walk. Its tail flicked above a scornful white rump. It crossed the road and, like the bison, descended out of sight, making for more private ranges below.

"I thought they lived in herds. This one is all on its own. Do you think it's sick?"

"Nah. You saw how it ran." X shaded his eyes, gazed down across the road as if he might still see the pronghorn. "He's just a loner."

An especially strong gust blew down from the mountain's peak. It rocked me on my feet, rocked me against X's body. The larks quieted for a moment, intent on clinging to their swaying perches.

"You know, I had convinced myself to leave the night before last. I thought I'd get on a bus and go back to Rexburg. Yesterday – that's when I planned to do it, right after you finished painting in Temple Square."

"Why?" X didn't sound surprised, only curious. So it didn't matter to him after all whether I stayed or left. I was, in the end, only

Baptism for the Dead

the ghost of Rebecca, just as I had thought.

He read the concern on my face; he rushed to soothe it. "I'm glad you stayed. But I figured you would. I only want to know why you thought of going back."

"You're not surprised that I even considered it, though. How did you know?"

"I admit I've never done anything like it before, but I figured it can't be easy to leave a marriage. Even a sham marriage. It's got to be even harder to leave a religion. I used to smoke." His hand, involuntarily, made a gesture, knuckles out, fingers extended toward his face, as if he held the sketched line of a cigarette, as if he held the idea of one. Old habits die hard. "It was hell to quit. The compulsion for just one drag – the need for it, right in the pit of my stomach, like being slugged – *pow* – the anxiety I felt without it – I can't explain. There were days when I knew it was crazy to think of picking up a cigarette or even going near somebody who was smoking, but my whole body wanted to anyway. And my mind – I was so unsettled all the time. I remember not being able to rest or think straight because all I could think about was how good a smoke would taste right then. You can understand rationally that a thing will destroy you, but there's a force inside you that will drive you back to it all the same."

The Nail in the Sure Place

"Maybe," I said. "Maybe that's what I was feeling. All I know for sure is that I felt like..." But I didn't know what I felt. I didn't know what I thought. Since we arrived in Utah I had not examined my feelings. Like an animal I had only sensed the discomfort, the threat, and wanted to flee back to whatever safety I might find in familiarity. Run back to your herd, lone creature. There is safety in numbers. "I felt guilty. A good woman gets married, and takes care of her husband, and has children, and takes care of them too. I felt I'd shirked my duties, I guess. I felt I needed to get back to being good."

X nodded. "But you didn't get on the bus. Why?"

I caught sight of movement in the distance, out on the plain below the road. The pronghorn, pressing on past the bison herd, shouldering through the tall grasses. I watched its progress for a long, quiet moment. "Everyone back home is so concerned with eternity. It's all anyone lives for. It's the focus of everything we do – *they* do. You study the scriptures. You tithe. You court. You marry and are sealed in the temple in an eternal partnership. You have children and you teach your family about eternity. You serve in the temple to earn points for eternity. You baptize the dead to give them hope for eternity. You worry that if you stole a pack of gum as a kid, or had a secret boyfriend, or don't participate in the Church enough, or feel unfulfilled in your marriage, that you will be demoted in eternity. You'll miss out on all the good stuff if you don't do it right, if you aren't perfect. I don't think I even believe in an eternity. I'd just been taught for so long to fear what might happen to me after I die, that I might not make it to the top...."

"That's a hell of a way to live, always preoccupied with where you'll go when you die."

"I watched you painting the temple yesterday, and I thought about the things people make. And I realized I've been so concerned with fitting in for so long that there was never any room in my head to wonder what it means, to not believe in God. What it means practically. Functionally."

"My own humble watercolor of a temple is responsible for all this deep thought? I'm flattered."

"It's like this. It took the pioneers forty years to build that temple. And it's beautiful – you saw it. They put so much skill into it. They put love into it. Some people must have worked on it knowing they would never live to see it completed. But they worked on it all the same. Forty years."

X lowered himself to sit on the boulder,

folded his lanky legs beneath him, waited for me to go on. I joined him. The surface of the rock was warm, minutely furred with lichen. I ran my palms over it. Bits of the boulder crumbled under my hands.

"People have this drive to make and make. We all want to leave something behind after we're gone – a painting or a song or a book. A baby; a temple. You turned the temple into something else, something all your own. You made your own temple. And the people who saw what you did with it – they'll remember. At least for a little while. Some of them will remember their whole lives. Some of them will see the picture you painted every time they look at the real thing. You altered the world, X.

You changed them."

His broad mouth turned a little, an uncertain smile, half flattered, half confused.

Oh, I am getting nowhere. Like a slug to the stomach, *pow*. "I think," I said carefully, hoping the words were right, hoping he understood, "that's the only afterlife we get. To make something that changes other people. Make a temple or a child – create something that has meaning to somebody else, and memory...."

"Memory is eternity."

"Memory and meaning. Changing a life. A

great work, whatever it is...I don't think there's a heaven. I think you were right about that. Now that I'm away from Rexburg I can really think about it, and I know, I *know* that this world is all we have. We only get one life. It's short." Even to myself I had never said these words. But they came to me like revelation. The simplicity of the words choked me, the beauty of them. I swallowed hard; my eyes burned with tears. X saw and took my hand, stroked my fingers with his callused thumb as if to comfort me.

But I did not need comfort. The realization of life's miraculous brevity filled me with a fire so hot I could not speak. I could only tremble inside, throb with the great burning pulse of it. This was the fire of the Holy Ghost, or so I had always been told – the surge in the heart that comforts, the shiver in the blood that assures. This was the thrum along the nerves, the spirit filled to brimming – but I have no spirit, and yet still I overflowed. I returned X's touch, rubbed my hand over his knuckles, over his wrist where the skin softened, as if to push the things I could not say through his skin and into his veins.

X, I do not know what happens after life. But I know that life is short, and life is this: larks on a hillside, and bison with diamonds in their eyes. A pronghorn tearing from its silent refuge, its hooves pounding in my heart. Life is the feel of your skin against mine, the smell of salt and grass on wind.

Life is the lightning flash that illuminates an ecstasy of love and hope and sorrow and loss; a blink, a breath, and nothing. But oh, the beauty of that flash, when all is lit bright enough to be seen, even the owl's tracks in the dust. And oh, the frailty of every heartbeat – how I treasure my heart now, like I never did before, like I never could before.

The pronghorn still moved, so far away now that the colors of its hide were barely discernible against the landscape. It moved past the caked, dried shore and out onto the gleaming white salt flats where at last it found its peace. Tiny, light-limned, it knelt to rest in the sun. I held tight to X's hand. I felt the beat of the pronghorn's hooves beneath his skin, where the veins tracked like rivers through the earth.

7.

Be fruitful and multiply, and fill the earth and subdue it. Have dominion over the fish of the sea, over the birds of the air, over every living thing that moves upon the earth.

You are raised to believe this and you believe it. When your world is Rexburg, with its potato plants in neat quilted rows, with its carousel under cover – when your world is so assured of its dominion, well, even the secret non-believer feels a thrill of pride at the sight of the earth subdued in plots and acreage. No, pride is not the right word. The bespoke arability of the Bench and the Basin, the brown land's fertility harnessed by the blood of intrepid pioneer men, the complacency of feed-lot cattle – these had filled me with a sense of this-is-right, a security and a foundation religion could not provide me. And I only realized now, going south and east, as the land we moved through shed its domesticity, that it was religion that built that sinkhole foundation after all.

Be fruitful and multiply; fill the earth and subdue it.

Utah's tamed circular fields gave way all at once to a great upward thrust of foothill and beyond that, through that, for that is where the highway led, the earth was not as docile

The Nail in the Sure Place

as God would have liked. The pass between two great mountains was a mess of color. On the western slopes, every available patch of earth clamored with olive-greens and pale blossoms, too scattered and frantic for my eye to categorize. Here and there the vertical thrust of some tall, stalky, thick-leafed plant waved a banner of yellow polleny bloom, its upward gesture distorted by our speed to a horizontal blur. We reached the summit of the pass, where we stopped for cold drinks at a lone boxy gas station, the only building for miles. Inside an enormous moose head hung over the cashier's counter, stiff and offended. I wondered where the cashier lived, why she bothered to commute all this way to the top of a lonely, wild pass with no one for conversation but the moose. We had passed no homes for at least forty miles and on the eastern slope it would be longer still until we caught the faintest whiff of a town.

As we pressed east the vegetation yielded to barer and redder ground. Every few miles stone fists the color of clay reared above flats of scrawny sage, and far in the purple distance, the plain slanted up at a piqued angle, a break at the edge of the world, the cracking of some long, slow catastrophe.

Fill the earth and subdue it.

How?

Baptism for the Dead

Subdue this great desert with its cunning, thorny life? How? Bring down the Tetons, fold them beneath the earth and build in their place a temple of gray stone and snow shadows, beautiful and straight between its walls but lacking the dangerous pitch, the hysterical cant of the highest peak, the dark scars in its face where solid rock has dropped away to fall like a cottonwood on a roof. Make a hundred thousand replicas of Devil's Tower, a forest of Chimney Rocks with valley views and modern amenities. Saddle a buffalo. Give him a name. It's all an illusion.

In pursuit of subjugation, the intrepid pioneers built a dam of slag and mud, years before I was born, across the great silver vein of the Teton River. Less than a year later the dam failed, and a wall of noise and fear and stench went right through Rexburg, without any regard for the dominion of its citizens. It killed unimaginable numbers of cattle, swept them in rafts past houses with crushed-in sides like kicked tin cans in a gutter. When the Teton River had had its fun and the waters receded, eleven people were dead and every house not up on the Bench was ruined. Foul-smelling mud full of rotting things coated the walls of houses, six feet high, eight feet high. The stink was astounding. The mud, I am told, was rust-red as dried blood, red as the desert through which X and I traveled, and it

The Nail in the Sure Place

stained everything – family photos, furniture, church floors. Homeowners painted over the stains only to see them reappear years later. The memory of the smell was in everybody's nostrils.

The one thing the flood could not permanently mark was the pioneering spirit of my hometown. Oh, what a wellspring of righteous pride, that we regrouped, rebuilt, found new ways to irrigate our tidy crops, kept on as God intended. What firm dominion we held, never doubting, never swaying. (The foolish man built his house upon the sand, and the rains came tumbling down.)

Subdue this earth, with its cottonwoods and windstorms, its falls of granite, its sudden herds of bison. There is a cant to the earth's horizon, a fierce angle, a caution to the wise. We drew ever closer to that horizon, X and I, deeper into the flood-red landscape. And I could see that in Rexburg we had it all wrong. Man cannot subdue. Man can never hold dominion over that which flies or that which springs from hiding on heartbeat hooves. Nor did I have any desire to bend a place to my will. My life is too short to live it with a whip in hand. I am the one who is subdued, and the mystery of the broken horizon is my master.

8.

This was a land as hot and red as slapped skin. We filled jugs with water at the park's entry gate, pressed on past popular sandy trails and scenic overlooks in search of lonelier vistas. The road carried us upward into a forcefully blue sky; ahead, great arches of rock formed eyes of sky that watched me as we passed. I stared back into them. They were bluer even than X's eyes. They turned to follow me until purple shadows blinked them closed.

Cool me, shadows. Comfort me, flood-red, in all my wasted places. Beyond the boundaries of the park, stretching out to a boundless view, the wilderness was Eden, the desert God's garden. Funny how even when you know it to be all backward, you still can't help but experience the world in terms of religion. X was never afflicted this way, having been raised without belief, so I could not tell him what it was like to feel the sharp edge of that contrast press against my heart, the boundary between what I know and what I had been taught as clear and opposing as sky against rock. What a tickle. I could not make him understand how humorous it was, that I felt the desert landscape in terms of Mormon poetry. This was Zion, after all, a place and a concept bred into my bones. *In the furnace God may prove thee, thence to bring thee forth more bright.* Oh, I have always been one for irony.

X found his lonely vista. High up near the park's altitudinal summit we came across an empty parking lot, a short trail through the brush, an unassuming fin of red sandstone rising from the desert as serene and ancient as a whale's back. Any rock fin is a miracle of geology far finer than the buttes and lava heaves Rexburg had on offer, yet compared to the cathedral towers and eyed arches of the rest of the park, this hike seemed to promise little. I wondered whether we might have more fun on a populous trail, tourists be damned. But X had set his heart on this simple fin.

I followed him across the sand. It worked its way through the seams of my shoes, through my socks; soon my toes were covered in soft, cool powder. The soles and fronts of my old white shoes stained orange.

The moment our trail rounded the fin my hesitation vanished. It was not one whale's back but two, standing close together broadside to the road. The brush gave out. Twin lines of placed stones and wood pieces indicated that our path continued between the fins, into a cool blue gap in the rock. We scrambled over a cracked hump of stone, our sneakers slipping and hissing.

Baptism for the Dead

Beyond the gap, with no warning, without even the flipping open of a hymnal, my heart ignited – my soul ignited, a fiery furnace. Katherine, this is what you felt when you entered the temple for the first time. At last I understood.

Red stone walls towered on either side; in the space between, X and I could have held hands and stretched out our arms to brush, just barely, with reverent fingers the formless friezes carved, all arcs and angles, down the length of the chapel. Time and weather printed these mysteries on this temple wall: thousands and thousands of winters bearing the slightest traces of snow, the water seeping into the rock, the expansion of the freeze, the strange hypnotic voice of cracking stone, a language I would never understand but which rang in my heart all the same. If angels existed, if they had their own tongue, it would sound like the break of erosion in a lonely place in a high red desert. I read the violet scroll-work of ages and I tried to imagine how many angels had spoken here. Uncountable years, uncountable voices.

Like a bright altar, a low, tenacious tree held fast to a boulder in the center of our temple – a mesquite, perhaps; I was too awe-struck to identify it. It spread across the expanse between the rock fins, defiant and beautiful, its leaves slender and fine and lit by a beam of sun that fell at just the right angle over the temple wall. Brilliant, mobile, living green, glowing, just on the verge of bursting into flame, just on the verge of singing to me in God's voice, how my legs trembled, how my heart burned with the fire of rapture. I fell on my knees in the sand to receive my blessing.

A wind had long since passed and softened and settled the sand, so that the footprints of those who came to worship before us were swept into shapeless anonymity. Across the implied path of a supplicant's feet the crisp recent tracks of some small dog-like animal cut, a fox or a coyote. Near the rock wall a small splash of its urine had not yet dried. This creature of the red temple had moved here like a ghost just moments before X and I appeared. I pressed my fingertips into the tracks of its toes.

"God," X said, an exclamation only. *Now that I have spoken these words, if you do not understand them it will be because you ask not, neither do you knock; and you are not brought into the light, but must perish in the dark.* Poetry, stood on its ear – on the furred, pointed, twitching ear of the holy ghost that detects the arrival of two pilgrims and vanishes. This flame that consumed me, that shook me – this was the spirit which brought me through the red sea on dry ground. With tears burning my eyes I followed X's gaze up into the sky. Above and between the temple walls, against a blue truer than prayer, a fast wind moved a layer of cloud thin as a veil. "God," X said again, and I nodded because I am human, and I laughed at the smallness of the word.

The Nail in the Sure Place

9.

In the town of Moab, in a busy grocery parking lot where mud-skinned Jeeps clustered together like cattle in a feed lot, I made a phone call.

James answered on the first ring. He was waiting to hear from me.

"It's good to hear your voice," I said.

"You too." He sounded happy, almost – lightened somehow. "I've been praying about this, everything we're going through."

"Oh?"

"I feel like it's going to work out."

X was inside the store, buying ice for our cooler and more food. He had brought in the travel mugs so he could wash out the old coffee staining their rims in the bathroom sink. He would be a while.

"I'm glad you're feeling better about things," I said carefully. "What do you mean by *work out?*"

"I know you're going to come home. We're going to be able to put this behind us and go on with our lives."

I knew if my silence stretched on too long he would be hurt. But all I could think to tell him was the truth: that I had seen and felt something greater than God, that a holier ghost had moved in me. That life was too short for Rexburg.

I did wait too long. He caught the hesitation. He said, "The Spirit told me." A rebuke.

"James, I'm not coming back."

In his pause I heard him tremble. I leaned my head against the car's window frame, watched a shadow of cloud, long and thin and fluent, glide across the face of the bluffs overlooking the town. You're cruel, I said to the red stone. You're cruel to reveal this truth to me. Now I can never go back.

"What do you mean?"

"I love you, James."

"Don't."

"I do. You don't know how much."

"Then why?"

"We need to do this for both of us."

"No." His broken voice, his painful voice. If I could have held him, begged his forgiveness. I just wanted to know that he didn't blame me. I hadn't done this to us. Don't blame me,

The Nail in the Sure Place

James, please; I can't bear it.

"I want you to be who you really are."

He said my name. It was thin and high, a bird's cry in the far distance, faint. The sound of it was

a nail through my heart.

"I'll make all the arrangements. I don't want to trouble you."

"What about our house?"

"We'll figure it out. I'll figure it out. I just want you to focus on you right now. How is Brian? Is he there with you now?"

James would not comment on Brian. "This can't be happening. This can't be real. The Spirit told me. I felt it. I was sure."

The Spirit is tracks in the sand, I told James silently. How I hated it, the idea of it, the myth, for wounding my husband. It lied to you, James. It never was there.

"Please understand, James. Please. I can't go back to that life. It's not me anymore."

"I don't understand. I'll never understand how you can want anything different from that life.

Anything else is not really a life."

"Life is what you make of it. Life is eternity."

"That doesn't make any *sense*." He spit the last word into the phone. It pounded in my ear.

The sky was dim blue, growing dimmer and grayer. The bluffs lost the glow on their skin; their faces turned sober gray-red, cold, the color of desert shadow.

"Please," I said again. "Try to understand. Talk to Brian. He loves you. I do, too. That's why I have to do this."

"I can't believe it," he said, stubborn, his voice steady with determination. "I believe what the Spirit told me. You will come home. I have faith."

"I know you do." And I had none. All I had was my longing for eternity and the feel of the red rock temple vibrating in my middle.

"I love you," he told me, as if the words were his hands on my head, a blessing to guide me home.

I hung up in time to see X striding out of the store, his long thin arms unswinging, laden with bags. I opened the door to help him pack the food into the cooler but he noted the look on my face. He put down his burden, right there in the parking lot, and pulled me to him. His shirt picked the tears off my cheeks, blotted them away. I pressed my eyes and my

The Nail in the Sure Place

nose against his chest and breathed deep so I would not sob.

"You did it, didn't you?"

I nodded as best I could, pressed up against him like that.

"It's going to rain," X said softly. "Rain in the desert." I pulled away from him. The sky was black and hot with thunder.

I said, business-like, "Let's get everything put away for we'll be outside the car when the lightning hits."

"You're going to be all right," he said. He sounded so assured.

With the thunder coming on, I knew the fox in the red stone temple would go to ground somewhere, curl itself into the purple cleft of a rock or push deep into the cool sandy earth in a burrow beneath a yucca. Tell me, I implored it. Tell me James will be all right. It was not a prayer. Not exactly.

10.

Somebody set the Grand Canyon on fire. Or the rim, at least. A camp fire jumped its metal ring. A cigarette butt out a window. The air stung our eyes. The smell of burning juniper trees filled our hair and clothing. We bought ice cream at a concessions building where men were busy installing a new roof – smell of the smoke, violence of the nail guns, punching the air, punctuating. We climbed the old stone watchtower and peered out its arched windows but the view was all fouled and obscured. The Colorado was a weak dirty snake twisting in the earth. The fire had advanced clear to the canyon's edge, a mile or more off to our left. Smoke poured over the rim and hung in the still air just below, to fill the gorge by degrees, inevitably. X said there might be a good sunset with all this smoke, but he didn't want to try to paint it. Too many people, too much noise. When we finished our ice cream we pressed on.

"Well, that was a disappointment," he said when the low, slumping plume of smoke that was the Grand Canyon finally disappeared behind us.

I watched it go, turned around in my car seat, twisted so hard my side ached like I had been running too long. I had hoped for a better view. The Grand Canyon was the big trip we took the summer of my thirteenth year. My dad was given a major contract and a bonus. We had a little extra for the first time in my young life, and a family vacation was in order – one of those memory builders, with the big rented white van that smells of hot vinyl and the cooler full of cans of pop and bologna sandwiches. Car songs: everybody sings on these vacations, as if the singular joy of moving and seeing can't be adequately expressed by regular conversation. My big brother taught us Boy Scout songs. Fish and chips and vinegar, vinegar, vinegar. We sang it in rounds. Mom's voice was as schooled and lovely as it ever was in church, warbling over her hymnal. She told me once that she could have been an opera singer but she decided to be a mom instead. I felt lucky.

At the Grand Canyon we camped and hiked and posed on the edges of rock walls for snapshots, and behind all these memories was a spectacular vastness of Creation, the land carved and painted just so, planned, a deliberate act of beauty just for me to enjoy with my kind siblings and my opera singer mother and my big-shot businessman father. I was so lucky; I was so blessed. It was the last time I can clearly recall feeling that way: that God had made it all for me, that God was a force of making, a friendly something in the sky that cared whether I enjoyed the view.

It was the summer before Adam. It was the last summer when I still believed. That the Grand Canyon was now a sullen stand of impersonal cliffs hiding behind smog, and a noisy crowd setting brush fires, and a crew of men with nail guns – it all seemed so tragically perfect. It made me laugh. X gave me his side-eye look that meant he'd pay a penny for my thoughts.

"The last time I was here it looked very different," I explained.

"It's the Grand Canyon. How different could it have looked?"

I told him about the car songs and the camping, and the feeling I still had back then that God had made it all for me. "You know, Rexburg isn't so bad." The words came from nowhere, from a pause to catch my breath, but they were right out before I had even thought them, voice on autopilot.

"Oh?"

"It's got something you can only find there – this conviction that a Creator spent so much time making the Grand Canyon just so that one day millions of years later *you* will stand at an overlook with your family and think, *Wow.*

The Nail in the Sure Place

It's stupid, I know, but that kind of simple view of the world...it's so *easy*. It's so comforting. I understand why James doesn't want to give it up. It feels so good to believe that you've got it all right, and your life will be perfect and you'll live forever in Heaven and be happy all the time."

"And all you have to do is play along."

"No. You have to believe. James believes. He thinks he can make himself into something simple and pure enough for Rexburg. But I don't want him to. That place is fine for the people who are already simple and pure. But James and me – we're not like them. We can't hammer ourselves into that mold."

"You can't decide that for him." X's words were gentle, not a reprimand.

"I know. But I can decide it for myself. The cruel thing is that without me, he has to remake himself all over again, or find someplace else to go – someplace just like Rexburg, where he can start the whole simple life over." Hiding all the while. "So if I don't go back and take up where I left off, I *am* deciding for him."

"So where do you want to go? What do you want to do?"

Highway signs and billboards whipped past us. The air inside the car still smelled faintly of juniper smoke. There as an echo of a nail gun inside my head. I thought of Rebecca, of the way her face was shaped just like mine, how her hands folded the way mine did. I couldn't go with X to Seattle. He was chasing his own ghost. He was not committed to me, but to his memories. And I – was I still looking for Adam? In Seattle I might find him. Perhaps after his parents' divorce he had put down roots there. Maybe on a street silver with rain our paths would cross, we'd catch one another's eyes, stop midstep, laugh at the shock of finding each other so unexpectedly, so far from where we first fell in love. On the streets of this city I had never seen, a city I imagined to be as reticent and gray as the Grand Canyon in smoke, we would erase the lost years between us. But no – no, X would be in Seattle, too. X and I both, proxies for one another's losses, crossing paths just as surely as I would with Adam, X and I chasing each other through the rain.

"I don't know what I want to do." For now I just wanted to build my memories. Life was short, and X, proxy or not, was here, and his leg was warm stone beneath my palm. Let's make a lighting strike together, X. Let's wire a circuit that will one day be a great wind in the Teton Valley. Let's tear down a whole forest of cottonwoods. "I know what I want to do. I want to teach you a song."

"A song?"

The Nail in the Sure Place

"It's a Boy Scout song. My brother taught it to me when we visited the Grand Canyon."

"Good. I don't know any Boy Scout songs yet."

X cranked the air conditioner against the afternoon heat. It raised the fine hairs on my arms. We sang in a round all the way across Arizona.

Veil

Veil

1.

X was determined to show me the Pacific Coast. We headed through the desert toward California, a place whose very name felt mythological. Our road cut across the neat angle of Arizona's northwest corner. The sun neared the horizon. The light was coral-flushed and fading as we descended into the Virgin River Gorge, deeply cut on one side by machines and dynamite. On the other side the river itself had done the cutting, tumbling and touching and smoothing red rock walls into rounded curves, the river like a potter's hands, wet and thick with mud.

We pulled into the entrance of a recreation area on the canyon's floor, drawn level with the crafty river – a boat launch, a sandy hiking trail. The absurd figure of a road runner skittered across the trail head, paused, bobbed its mohawked head and blinked at us with its glaring yellow eye. "Meep meep," X said. It disappeared into a tangle of thorns, too dignified to respond. Cholla bushes stretched their fishnetted, jagged arms this way and that. The air was still plenty warm, though sunset was not far off. We followed the trail down to the place where red water flashed and stirred past boulder and brush.

We removed our shoes and socks, piled

them atop a flat purple stone. The floor of this place was red sand, soft as skin – the walls of the canyon worn and worn and cast down grain by grain. I wondered how many years of the river's life each grain represented. I wondered, and I pushed my toes deep into the sand. A buried twig pricked me. The walls of the canyon were streaked with great slashes of violet-black, banded vertically as if stained by falling water, as if the gorge had recently wept its makeup onto its sorrowful face. But of course there was no falling water here, and what could anyone cry over in a place such as this?

Where the river arced gently against the shore the sand had turned to mud. The mud was tepid, blood-colored, imprinted with the feet of shy animals. I stepped carefully through the tracks, sometimes raising up on my toes so that I would not erase a single one. I paused to see where my feet fell, the proof of my passing woven into the lace of deep, sharp, delicate prints of deer, the skewed pad-marks of a coyote, the incised primitive cuneiform of birds' feet. In a million years, I told myself, these prints will harden and some future archaeologist will wonder what I was doing here, a human coming down to the river to drink with the wild things. But of course with the next rain up in the mountains the creeks would swell, the Virgin River would rush and rise and fill all our tracks with bits of canyon.

Veil

We never were here. The thought made me smile – precious, impermanent tracks in mud. That we had proof, even for a few hours, that a deer passed this way on legs like lovers' fingers, that a deer *was* at all – and that *I* was, barefoot and anonymous to this gorge....

I waded into the river up to my ankles. It pulled at my skin. Beside me, a splash: X rolled the legs of his jeans up past his wooly knees and strode into the river, taking more and more of it with each step. It hit his calves, rippled around his legs, his knees. "You're going to get wet," I called to him, but he only laughed and went deeper. Thigh deep, waist deep, until the end of his shirt drank up the red muddy tinge of the river, until his skin was soaked in river. He turned back to look at me. He laughed again, loud, his mouth wide as my heart. The warmth of sunset flashed like a fire under his skin, illuminating him, making him glow until I felt the heat of him against my face, though my ankles were still in the shallows and he was there, staggering and laughing in the current.

What a rare thing, that interval of time between the moment when the sun touches the horizon and the moment the sky cools and darkens. How bright and special is the light just then, how low and warm, how sweetly it speaks. How many times in my life would I see it? How many times would the sun set on X in the middle of this river, soaked and glowing,

Baptism for the Dead

laughing? I had only seconds to live this. And because I had only seconds, the present filled my hands with a weight like gold. What good is eternity? Let the river rise. Let the canyon wear. Let the tracks wash away. I saw you laughing in the river, X. What is heaven beside that?

2.

We were nearly an hour into the Mojave night when my phone rang. I pulled it from my purse and stared numbly at the name on the screen: *Mom-Dad*. My veins turned sluggish and cold. The phone kept ringing. X glanced at the phone's screen, at me, turned back to the road. I let it go to voice mail, and gripped the phone tightly as though I might squeeze something out of its hard plastic electrons, some meaning behind the fear that clutched at my bowels and heart so suddenly.

Why should a call from my family chill me? I sorted it with ponderous care. My thoughts moved like hands under water, dragging, wavering, too slow to keep up. In the same instant that my voice mail indicator beeped it came to me.

"The whole time I've been gone from Rexburg, no one in my family has called me." X nodded.

"They pretended nothing happened, like I never left."

X said nothing, watching the road with a face that was too calm for real calm. He knew something was wrong as surely as I did. The voice mail was too hasty for this call to be an extended olive branch. There was something terse and dutiful about it. There was some vast unpleasantness here, something best gotten over with quick.

X pulled over.

The desert was pallid and cold under the blue-white light of the moon. Brittle clumps of some weedy, sickly grass shivered in a constant small wind. Beyond the shoulder of the road the ground was crusted with white pebbles, hard as asphalt. X switched on the hazard lights and followed me out into the darkness, away from the road. I walked until my phone showed just one bar of signal, and then I called my mom and dad.

Mom answered. It had been so long since I'd heard her voice that the sound of it choked me. She sounded tired, distressed, not pleased to hear from me.

"The police came by our house because they couldn't find you," she said. Her voice was at war with itself. Something in her wanted to push me away and something wanted to draw me close and rock me.

"Don't tell me." I didn't want to hear these words.

She sighed, and there was a pause, and I could see her, so clearly, drawing in a breath

Veil

and holding it, her face fighting to stay calm but crumpling anyway, the way it had done when she told me Grandpa died, the way it had done one night when I found her crying alone in my parents' bed, my father gone from the house.

Then she coughed out a little sob, a tiny, confused sound.

"Tell me."

Hands gone useless. Clutching the phone so tight, so I would not drop it into the desert, so it would not fall through the hole opening below me in the cold hard earth.

"Oh, honey...James is dead. They found him in the river in Idaho Falls."

Not real. Real was the slant of the distant mountains, bright blue in the moon. Real was the noise the dry plants made in the wind, in my silence, in my mother's silence. I reached out my free hand as if I might touch a mountain, brush some of the blue light off its flank with my stiff fingers. X took my hand, held it hard, squeezed until it felt real, and painful, and real.

"What happened?" There were tears in my voice. My eyes were hot. Was I crying now? Water runs down the red rock wall to stain it in vivid purple bands.

"He took his own life. He shot himself in

Baptism for the Dead

the chest. You have to come back to Rexburg. How soon can you get here? You have to come back so we can plan his funeral."

Our car on the shoulder looked very far away. Its hazards flashed, rhythmic and mindless, a rapid heartbeat; the light stained my eyes in reverse, so that for every orange beat of the heart a blue echo blinded me, blotted out the desert and the sky and the phone in my hand, nothing but a blue glow and a hot lit heart. I told my mother yes, of course I would come back, I would be back soon. We would have a funeral for James. I would come home.

*

And then X is picking up my phone from the white pebbles on the ground, and my vision is full of blue blood stains, and I howl, doubled over, pressing my fists into my stomach. A semi like a windstorm passes us and screams, the great throat of its horn open and wailing. The sounds bends around me like a steel bar.

3.

The sky filled with cloud, in bands like the stripes on the canyon wall, ripples in a puddle. We were...somewhere. Somewhere, Utah, innumerable somewheres with perfect homes on the hills and white steeples every half mile, someplace where everyone played their part, everyone did as they should. We drove fast. We passed these places by.

Far outside a town it began to rain. A skinny girl on a spotted horse galloped alongside our car, right on the edge of the highway. Her young body moved with a strength and confidence, a familiarity with the muscle and flow of the animal's gait. How beautiful, I thought, and then I hated myself for thinking of beauty now. How could I think of anything now but how cold it is in the Snake River? I had never held a gun but I imagined it felt cold, too, and awkward, pointed at your own heart, clumsy and slow.

Dimly I realized that now was the time when I should pray; this was the time when people prayed, when the world blew down, when the tree cracked the roof and cleaved the house in two. Why did this happen? I asked God. What is your plan? There must be a plan. There must be a reason. What are you for unless there is a reason? What good are you without a plan?

I watched the hooves of the horse pounding and the whip of the girl's black braided hair, and the flaring of the red-rimmed nostrils as the horse, straining, fell behind us and we pulled ahead.

There was no one there, no reason. There was only a flash – a flash of sunset on a river, a flash from the muzzle of a gun. And then, too soon, gone.

It was raining.

We passed these places by.

*

Wheat plains and potato fields. Lava heaves, cracks in the yellow ground, black fissures. My dad used to tell me how, as a boy, he and his friends would take their BB guns out into the lava heaves and play war. All day long they crouched down in the natural trenches and shouted insults at one another, and fired their guns at each other's hiding places. "It's a wonder we never put out any eyes," he said. Those gangs of spindly boys with their sun-browned arms and the backs of their necks burned red, cutting their knees on the sharp bits of basalt littering the trenches. Generations of Rexburg boys down in the earth, shouting, bleeding, shooting pellets to ping off the rocks. If I had stayed put, if James and I had had our children, our boys might have done the same. Or they may have grown up like their Daddy, sweet and soft and intelligent. I couldn't imagine James in the trenches, roughhousing with other boys. That was not him. The reader, the quiet, good boy, the one who went to seminary school every morning, bright and early – that was my James. Those were the boys we would never raise.

Like a body inhaling, the Bench lifted up out of the earth, rib cage expanding, slowly ascending from the horizon, and from the road I could already make out the temple, waiting, and the bright speck of the Teton peaks behind it, dreaming.

Except for the missionaries, I must have been the only one who had ever left Rexburg and come back again.

Baptism for the Dead

4.

Rexburg in the dark, the broad streets a flat gunmetal blue by night, checkerboarded by the orange glare of streetlights. Shade trees standing very still. My hands turned the steering wheel easily, smoothly, knowing the way though my mind had gone as blank as pavement. I crossed Main, passed beneath the shadow of the hospital, swung onto Ricks Avenue unthinking, rolled to a stop outside the white silence of my parents' house. I had been all business at my own home, helping X to carry in our bags, lying down in the guest room at his insistence to get some rest, which evaded me as I stared at the ceiling, but X had told me to rest and I had given it my best effort. Composed and matter-of-fact, I moved about my empty house as I had moved about countless hotel rooms, doing what needed to be done, knowing I would not stay long. Now, though, as I sat looking at my childhood home from the quiet of X's car, the familiarity of the place undid me. I trembled. The house was as I had always known it, its clean siding rising clear of the bare foundation, its two garage doors dozing and closed, the pots of flowers on the porch steps in full bloom as they always were, no matter the season.

I remembered sitting on the cool concrete

Veil

of those steps in the summertime, reading my Book of Mormon. I would always remember. I would always be there, the feel of the cold steps delicious in the sun, with the book open in my lap. My name was embossed on the cover of that book – a baptism gift from my parents. Inside the book, Mom had affixed a single mustard seed with clear tape and she had hugged me and told me with pride in her voice, "Heavenly Father said, even if you have faith as tiny as a mustard seed, you can move mountains." I remember standing in the hallway of our church with neighbors and friends moving all around me, congratulating me, squeezing my small shoulder with warm hands. My hair was still wet from the baptismal font. I felt the weight of the Scriptures in my hands, admired the clean new cover of the book, light purple to appeal to an eight-year-old. The gold script glimmered with my name. I felt how much they loved me then – my parents, and all the rest, everyone. I thought they must love me still, in spite of everything. I hoped they loved me still.

A dark figure approached the living room window, looked out at me. I knew from the shape and the briskness of movement that it was Marlee, my little sister. And the two cars in the driveway – my two older brothers, Cameron and Todd. Mitchell, the youngest, would not be here. He was in

Baptism for the Dead

Guatemala for another year, serving his mission, making new converts for the Church. He would have heard already. They would have given him the awful news. I felt a tremor of gratitude in my chest, that all of them were here, that even Mitchell was grieving with me. But it was Marlee I wanted to see most. She leaned her forehead against the window and I could make out the shadow of her face. She raised a finger and tapped a little rhythm on the glass, the secret knock we had always used to communicate, just us girls. I swallowed hard and went inside.

*

These are the times when a family draws together. I cried freely on my father's shoulder, hiding my face in the flannel of his shirt, in the unchanging scent of him, sawdust and cheap aftershave and all the flavors of my mother's cooking, and as I cried into him they all took turns holding onto me, too, my brothers, my sister, my rigid, torn mother who had been so proud of me, long ago when I was small. We tried to eat the dinner she'd fixed, all of us picking at it in silence, Marlee and I sitting so close together our shoulders touched. And when at last we gave up I excused myself and crept up the stairs to my old bedroom.

5.

It had been converted into a sewing room and my mother's quilts in various stages of creation were everywhere, folded on her work table, stretched taut on a wooden rack. But my bed was still there, narrow, neatly made with my collection of stuffed rabbits gathered among the pillows. A book case still stood, too, and there among my mother's sewing references and a scattering of advice books, no-nonsense for women, were the novels I had loved as a child and my old book of Scripture with its purple embossed cover. I pulled it out and sat on my bed, but I felt no desire to open it. I only held it, and squeezed the soft cover, felt how the pages compressed and heard their mild paper-on-paper groan.

The familiar rhythm tapped at the door. "Come in," I said to Marlee.

She edged into the room shyly and stood looking at me, a sad, sympathetic half-smile on her face. "That was a horrible dinner," she said.

"Mom tried."

"Nobody can eat at a time like this."

I looked at her, just twenty-three, pretty in that wholesome way we all had, the Rexburg girls, bright and funny and loving. When she was a baby I knew she would be mine forever, my little doll of a sister, and I loved her with a fierce, towering love. I remembered holding her tiny soft hands and gently flexing each finger in turn, comparing them to my own, how much bigger I was than she. Now there was a new ring on her finger, and she was probably already trying for babies of her own.

"Thank you for coming," I told her. "I'm glad you're here."

She sat beside me on the bed. "I'm sorry this happened to you. I'm sorry for James, too. I'm sorry for all of it. I know you love him, and I love him; he was my brother. But I never understood why he married you."

"He wanted to do the right thing."

"He was never doing anything wrong." She gave a small, rueful laugh. "Don't tell anybody I said that. You know what they'd all think of me. I'd never be allowed to bring a casserole to Relief Society again."

I smiled, grateful for the humor, for her understanding. "James did love me," I said. "I believe that. If he could have made the perfect life with anyone, it would have been me. I understood him better than anyone else in the Church could have."

"I know." She was sober now.

Veil

Perhaps it was her flip remark about casseroles, or her opinion of my husband. Or perhaps it was only because she was Marlee, and she was mine. All at once, I felt safe in telling her. "Mar, I don't believe in God."

"I guess not, at a time like this."

"No. I haven't for a long time."

She thought about this for a while, gazing down at the Scriptures in my lap. "Will you ever again?"

"I don't think so."

"That makes me sad," she said, simply.

"Why?"

"I worry what will happen to you. When you... when you die."

I hugged her. Beneath my hands I felt the seams of her temple garments, the insistent little ridges of them rising through her t-shirt. "Don't worry about me. I'm not worried about me. I'm more worried about you."

"Me?" She pulled away from me. Through the woman's features I still saw the baby's face, Marlee looking up at me with her sweet, solemn, dark eyes. Fragile as my emotions were, the great scouring flood of love I felt for her then rendered me nearly mute with its power.

Baptism for the Dead

"I'm going away after the funeral," I said, my voice hardly more than a whisper. "I wish you wouldn't stay in Rexburg, either. I wish you wouldn't stay in the Church. I think you're better than this place. I want more for you."

"Sis-sis." That special name, the one she'd given me when she was just a baby. "Leaving's not for me. I love the Church. It's got a few flaws, I know, but I love it. I believe in it. I wish you'd come back to it. But even if you never do, I still love you just as much as I ever did. And you're always my sister. You'll always be my best friend, no matter where you go." She stood and kissed my forehead and left my room, casting one final look at me that was overflowing with love.

I flipped open the cover of my Scriptures. The mustard seed was still there, small and hard, held in place by the yellowing, brittle tape. I picked at the tape; it crumbled in my fingers. I held the seed up and examined it in the light. It had changed not at all since the day my mother had given me the book. I pinched it, felt its hardness dig into my fingertips until the skin blanched white, until the seed left small indentations in my flesh. Then I put it into my mouth, held it between my teeth, and finally swallowed it. The taste it left on my tongue was as dry as dust.

Veil

*

I wandered out into the garden. The air smelled fresh and green in the summer night, burdened with the presence of so many growing things. I held my breath as a car passed by, driving slowly. In the silence that followed I thought I could just hear the distant, endless watery hiss of the irrigation canals edging the fields north of town. There was a small gazebo in my parents' garden, surrounded by hollyhocks taller than me. In the darkness the plants were as black as iron spikes. I crept into the gazebo. It had been our play house when we were children, all of us gathering there, launching our adventures out across the lawn. I sat on the gazebo's rail and watched my brothers helping Mom with the dishes. Framed by the window, bathed in warm light, they moved together like the parts of a clock, precise and ordered, cooperative, useful. Cameron side-stepped as Mom turned with a stack of plates, avoiding a collision, and their mouths opened in brief laughter. Todd dried his hands and hugged Mom, kissed her on the cheek. I felt removed, observational, distant.

The back door opened, throwing out a long beam of the house's warm inner light. My father came out into the yard, into my green-smelling outland. He shut the door quietly and peered into the darkness of the gazebo.

"Hey, Scamp."

"Hey, Daddy."

He made no move toward me, only put his hands into the pockets of his trousers and rocked on his heels. Did he not see me? Was he unsure where I was hiding? Out beyond the lawn, where my mother's flowers grew in a tangle, an old wooden gate stood dispossessed of any fence. My father had told us, growing up, that the gate had been there since the pioneer days and was a genuine relic. We all chose to believe that. I left the black cave of the gazebo and made my way to the gate, stepping carefully among the clumps of petunias gone to seed, the dahlias propped upright against stakes, the fists of their infant blooms curled tight. Daddy followed me.

The gate was rickety and dry. It had been painted white once, long ago; fragments of paint still clung to it here and there and stuck to my hands as I climbed onto it, one foot on its lower rail, ribs leaning across the top, and swung on it gently as I had done many times before. Dad and I used to talk here, just the two of us, when dinner was finished and the evening was drawing in. *What are they teaching you in that school of yours?* I recalled him asking, teasing. *Are they teaching you that the world is*

Veil

round? Hogwash. It's flat.

"We've been hearing things about you," he said. His hands were still in his pockets. "We heard you left town with another man."

The hinge of the old gate squealed. I swung slowly toward him. I did not want to talk about X. This was not about X. It was about everything else, everything that had led to X, and to Brian, too. It was about camouflage and the shedding of garments like dry snake skin. It was about the way we all chased illusions, promises, eternity, lost lovers. It was about driving out into the sage flats on a quarter tank of gas. Everything but X.

"A long time ago," I said, "I woke up in the middle of the night and found Mom crying. You weren't anywhere in the house. Where were you that night?"

His head dropped, his eyes deeply shadowed in the darkness, searching for something down among the shot petunias. I swung backward into the rustling foliage.

"You're right," he said. "It's none of my business."

We were both quiet for a time. I thought of all the ways he used to tease me, pulling quarters from behind my ears, making so many bad puns that all of us, even Mom, would groan and beg him for mercy. I wished he'd tease me now, but of course it was not the time for teasing.

"I'm sorry, Scamp," he said. "I'm sorry about what's happened. You're always my girl."

"Thank you, Daddy. Let's go back inside."

I held his hand as we crossed the lawn together. I saw how he looked into the house's windows the same way I had, a distant spectator, a lone, longing audience.

Inside, I gathered my purse and the keys to X's hybrid. "I need to get some sleep," I told my family. "There's a lot to do tomorrow."

"I assumed you'd want to stay here," Mom said, leaning against the archway that led into the kitchen. "You don't want to stay all alone at your house. Not after what's happened."

I would not be alone, of course. X waited there for me, though how long he would wait I did not know. Surely I had proven myself a troublesome partner, with my poor dead husband and my uncut ties to my hometown. I was no Rebecca at all.

"I'll be all right. I'd rather be in my own home tonight."

Mom followed me out to the car. I did not look back at her as I walked stiffly down the drive to the curb, but I felt the weight of her angry presence pushing into my back, hurrying me along.

"Is that man at your house?" she said as I unlocked the car door. "Is that why you're going back there?"

I did not answer.

"You have no respect at all. No respect for the dead."

I turned to look at her. Her loathing for me twisted her face, filled her eyes with a cold rage that stabbed at my center.

"I always thought you were better than this," she said. "I thought you would always do the right thing. You disappoint me. You disappoint God."

"I don't believe in God."

"Maybe it's better that way. God doesn't believe in you."

I got inside and slammed the door, grateful for the barrier between us. As I hurried away down the street, I could see my mother in the rear-view mirror, standing immoveable in the street, staring after me. Her figure grew smaller and smaller until I turned the corner. And then she was gone.

6.

The next morning Katherine invited me to her place for tea and cookies and funeral planning. Her children were off with their father, off at the park or the library or the movie theater so that we could do what needed doing in peace. Before I left for Katherine's I slipped the old tarnished CTR ring into the pocket of my jeans. It was my talisman, something concrete to touch when the world began to feel vaporous and shifty, as it did now so often. When I reached her home and felt wobbly from its familiar, pleasant smell, the remembered way the door creaked as it opened, I put my hand into my pocket and poked the tip of my little finger in and out of the ring.

Katherine was tearful and sympathetic. She hugged me. I clung to her and breathed deep, the smell of her clean hair and her tasteful perfume, so that I would not cry. I thought she would be too tactful and schooled to mention X. But straight away she asked the question that was surely on the lips of the entire town, and straight away my guts clenched and I knew I would find no peace here after all.

"Did you really leave town with some man?"

"It's more complicated than that. It's not really something I want to go into."

Veil

Sweet Katherine with her distant eyes. She sat so carefully on her sofa and sipped so nicely at her tea. "Of course. I'm sorry. You're so upset right now. We all are. It's not the time to talk about it." I picked up a brochure from a funeral home, one of the small handful Katherine had thoughtfully rounded up, doing the busy work so I wouldn't have to. It was so like a good woman to think these things through, to ease the burden off her neighbors. I was grateful, truly; this simple gesture of her concern for me brought fresh tears to my eyes. I had never managed to make myself into what she was.

Katherine misunderstood my tears. She rushed in to comfort me. "It's not your fault, you know. I hope you don't think so."

There was not enough conviction in her voice to assure even herself. I could see that when I looked up into her face. Pretty, pretty Katherine, with the lines of strain and motherhood already starting to show on her forehead, at the corners of her nose. I had never had many close friends in Rexburg, but Katherine was the closest. I had allowed her to know me better than anyone else, save for my husband. If she thought I was to blame for James's death, then the whole town did, too. It was already hard enough that I suspected they were right. I could not face a funeral full of townspeople who thought I had, in effect anyhow, pulled the trigger.

Baptism for the Dead

"I'd better take these and do what I can do on my own," I said, gathering up her papers and pamphlets. She protested weakly, but I showed myself out. Her relief at my going rushed out the door almost as fast as I did; I could feel it brush my skin. She had done her duty as my Visiting Teacher. She had offered what help she could stand to offer. She had honored our friendship, such as it was, enough to concern herself with an adulterer. That was more than plenty for both of us.

Visiting Creature, James's voice said inside my head. The sound of him was so sharp and present that I stopped in the middle of Katherine's walk, clutched at my stomach as if he might be in there, somewhere in the vicinity of the mustard seed. As if his actual voice had vibrated up through the earth, through the black lava fissures, through my bones and into my body. To hear his voice when I knew he was gone shocked me more than any other experience, more electric than the sight of X in the booth at Sombrero's, running the butter knife along his tongue. In a moment I realized it was only a memory,

that James had not spoken to me from the Celestial Kingdom, robed in white. Synapses in my tired brain had misfired and tickled alive the ghost of the sound of my husband. These were bits of him, the atoms, the electricity. James was laughing in the memory, laughing

Veil

with relief as our Visiting Teachers left our house. *Until next time*, James intoned, his eyes shining, his arm around my waist. In the middle of Katherine's walk I tipped my head back so the tears ran down to pool in my ears, and I laughed along with him. I slipped the ring off and on my finger.

I could not go straight home. X would wonder why I had been away for such a short time when there was planning to do, and I didn't want to talk about Katherine, about the town's inevitable suspicion that I had driven my husband to suicide. Instead I drove to the Dairy Queen where James and I had often sat during our three months of courtship, eating sundaes, discussing books. But I could not go in, couldn't even make myself leave my car. Instead I settled for a convenience store, where I bought a pack of grape bubblegum. This I slid into my pocket and walked up the hill to the college.

The college library was nearly deserted, but a few summer students huddled in groups over the long tables, smiling over stacks of books, whispering. I wandered deep into the stacks, alone in the cool light with the smell of paper and binding, the smell of James. I let my hand run along the spines of books as I walked, felt their leather surfaces and covers in plastic protectors that crisped faintly beneath my fingers, a wistful sigh of a sound. Too many books that James had never read. When I grew tired of walking I sat, right on the floor with the shelves stretching above me, somewhere in the 212 decimals. I asked James, Now what?

At first he didn't answer. But then he said, quietly, *Now I fall apart. Now I transform.*

I put a piece of gum in my mouth. I sat by myself in the brown light of the shelves, blowing bubbles and popping them and breathing in the air that had been inside, sweeter than any real fruit could ever be. On my way out of the library I paused beside the bronze bust of Rexburg's town founder, gazing sternly out the library door. Without even looking to see who might be watching, I pulled two bits of gum from my mouth and stuck them into the holes of his pupils. His eyes lit up, purple, staring. His face at once came alive.

It's an improvement, James said.

I agreed.

7.

When I returned to my house on the Bench the smoke of the farmers' fires in the valley below had just begun to rise. I walked through the side yard, ducked under the crab apple. The grass had grown long, though not as long as it should have grown in the weeks I had been away. Somebody, some kindly neighbor who wished no ill on me or on James, maybe Marsha's father, had taken it upon himself to cut it in our absence. In the back yard I stood with my arms folded and watched the columns of smoke ascend to heaven. Rexburg was a tidy, soft blanket laid over the slope of the land. The children who lived on streets lower down still made the most of their summer, flashing through yards between fences on bicycles or skates, bright blue and apple red, calling from swing sets. Surely some of them, the older ones, knew already that the nice professor who lived at the top of the hill had died. They played the afternoon away all the same. I longed to join them, running, yelling, outrunning all of this, passing it by. Insects buzzed in the long weeds at the rear of our lot. A dog barked. Soon a milder sound drew my attention, a repeating sound but not rhythmic, quiet; yet it filled my ears to the exclusion of all the rest, traveling up by bones: the creaking of my knees as I wavered where I stood. *You're tired*, James seemed to say. *You'd better go inside. Get some rest.*

Inside. X had been inside the house all day, laying low. In the mudroom I kicked off my shoes, just as I did that day when I first met him, when he dropped his business card into my purse and walked away grinning. I set the funeral home papers on the exact spot on the kitchen counter where James used to leave me his notes.

X sat in an easy chair near the bay window, the natural light falling across his face, limning the edges of his short dark beard with a halo of white. He looked apologetic when he glanced up at me, his eyebrows raised and knitted, his ankle crossed on one knee, his sketch pad resting shyly on the triangle of his bent leg.

"What's the matter, X?"

"I hope you don't mind. I never knew him, except for that one time we met, when you and I left town together. I was looking at some of the pictures on your wall, and...."

I approached. He held the sketch pad up to me, timid, afraid I would be angry at the intrusion. But oh, the sweetness of what I saw. Page after page of James alive, precise and known, and flawless and beautiful, exactly as he was.

Veil

*

You drew him, X. You saw him. You moved through the home we had shared and looked into my husband's face. You looked at the pictures on our walls, of James smiling with his arms around my waist, me in my sleeved bridal gown, James in his crisp suit, the temple white and straight behind us. You looked at James as a younger man, capped and gowned and clutching his scroll, his mother tucked under his arm and a future on his face. You looked at him in frames, in albums, in loose photos in drawers. James grinning at a ball game, James asleep on a car ride, James unaware the camera was trained on him, looking off into the distance with the weight of something hidden inscribed in the lines on his face. Every James I had ever known lived again on your pages, quicksilver lines, real.

I was no ghost to you. I knew it now. How could I have doubted? I saw the image, and knew it was the last time I would see it, of Adam picking his shirt up from the pavement. His glasses flashed white in the sun. He was growing faint around the edges. When I blinked the tears from my eyes the boy was gone. You were there with your sketch pad. I put my hand into your hair and felt how warm you were, warm and solid, just like me.

*

"Can you paint him?" I asked, kneeling beside the chair, my voice weak. "I want to see him again in color."

X said, "I can."

We worked on the painting for hours, together, first in the clean clear light of day streaming through the view window, filtered and colored only slightly by the smoke of the fires, then by lamp light as the moon rose. X started it over many times. Each time he determined the portrait had gone wrong, he sent me off to the bath tub to stretch new sheets of watercolor paper on his drawing board, soaking the sheets and holding them up to drip down into the water, taping them down, sponging them until they were barely damp. The repetitive work soothed me. And X was determined to capture perfectly the subject in all its beauty and complexity. He knew he hadn't yet got James right, because he asked me, talked all the time about James, listened as I told him how my husband's mouth had curved up more at the corners, how this small bit of hair over his ear had always stuck out

Veil

and he could never make it lie flat. We worked late into the night, and when at last I saw the James I had known, and when X was pleased with the delicacy of color and the accuracy of line, we crept into the guest bed we had shared weeks ago, in another lifetime.

What do you think? I asked James.

Pretty good.

I would give you more if I could.

I know.

This is it, you know. This is the afterlife. You've gone to pieces and electricity, and X took your energy and turned you into something that will live forever. Seems kind of inadequate, compared to what we all expected – the white place, and all that.

I know.

What else are you now, James? Besides just this painting?

I am wind and lightning, he said. *I am red rocks in the desert. I am the holy ghost, the tracks you find in the sand.*

Is it my fault? Did I do this to you?

James did not answer. I pressed myself against X's side and tried to sleep.

8.

The painting sat on an ornate easel surrounded by bouquets of lilies and hollyhocks and the casket where James lay still. In the glass over the portrait I saw the squares of the overhead lights glowing dimly, slanted, the faces of mourners shrouded by reflection, featureless and all the same.

My mother had scowled when I brought the painting in. I asked the funeral director for something to put it on.

"The whole town knows you ran off with an artist," Mom said quietly, tensely. No mourners had arrived yet except for my parents and me; there was no one to hear her words, but the shame of them compelled her to keep her voice down. "There's no need to rub it in our faces." The easel arrived. I thanked the director and ignored my mother.

"That doesn't belong here," she said, louder now, in a tone of weighty disapproval that would have terrified me once.

"Leave off, Karen," Dad said, and helped me straighten the portrait on its stand.

Mom tried to take the painting down. I seized her wrist and held it hard, looked her in the eyes with a strength that surprised me. She

Veil

retired to her seat and refused to look at me.

"Take it easy," Dad said quietly. I recalled the look of the back of his head as he drove the van out of the Grand Canyon. I recalled the smell of juniper smoke in his clothes, the sound of nail guns. No – that was another time, another visit. Fish and chips and vinegar, vinegar, vinegar. I had to keep the memories straight or else the afterlife would be confused, a maze I could never follow.

Throughout the service I sat beside my family in the front row and watched the portrait of James for signs of life. The curve of his mouth, perfect. The light in his laughing eyes. The shape of him, the delicacy of color. We stood and sang the songs. Eventually my mother slipped her cool hand into mine, and I held it and squeezed, accepting what little peace she could offer. Over the general chorus I heard Katherine's bright voice rise and soar, and I wondered at the thing she said to me days ago at her home. *It's not your fault. I hope you don't think so.*

It seemed every person in Rexburg had come to the service in their Sunday best, eyes wide with shock, though the capacity of the parlor was only two hundred and fifty. It was more than I could bear to accept all that sympathy, yet I could not leave. I was James's wife. I belonged here. So I stood and shook the men's hands

Baptism for the Dead

and put my arms around the women, and said words that must have sounded right, for no one looked at me more askance than to wonder why I'd done it, why I'd left such a good man who had only wanted to do the right thing. I went on shaking hands and hugging and speaking; my eyes recalled the backward flash of the hazards on the distant desert highway. Blue bouquets of light obscured the faces of the people I spoke to. Inside my head I was already far away, already leaving, driving down a long stretch of inviting highway that curved toward an unseen destination. Afterward there would be a potluck in the gym of the church, the one where James and I had played our roles. Feed all the hungry mourners. I would not be there.

His sisters and his mother were the hardest. I clung to them and wept, and one of them, I don't know who, whispered in my ear, her breath hot and thick with grief and absolution, "It's okay. I love you. I love you."

At last no more hands were offered. I was alone. The funeral director drifted into the parlor with an empty trash bag, and, business as usual, bent over a garbage can to change out the liner. She saw me and blushed, scuttled out again. A pause, the smell of lilies and the ticking of a wall clock, and X entered the room, stood with his arms out, waiting for me. I moved to him, navigating blindly around empty chairs. I pressed into his chest. He was as firm as stone and as warm as the desert. He was there. I let my tears fall onto his shirt. I soaked it, as it had been soaked by river water; my sorrow lay all across his skin, but he didn't seem to mind. He was there. How could I ever have thought he had Adam's eyes? They were his own, bright and loving and seeing everything, everything.

"Look," X whispered after I had cried against him for a long, long time.

I raised my head and by instinct turned to face the front of the parlor, where the portrait stood. A man approached it timidly. We watched, hardly breathing, as the man gazed at James, hands in the pockets of his well-pressed trousers. His shoulders were hunched. He was short, thin; his orange hair was curly and too long for Rexburg, too shaggy. It was mussed, too, flattened on one side, evidence of a sleepless night and a distracted morning, the kind of morning where one can spend so much energy ironing the perfect crease into trousers but can't bear to look at one's own face in the mirror. "That man is not from around here," said Katherine's voice, or mine. I did not see this man at the service, did not shake his hand or receive his sympathies as the line of townspeople filed out the door. I would have remembered him. Like X, he had stayed outside until the coast was clear. And then I knew him – of course I knew him, though we had never met before.

Baptism for the Dead

When he raised his hand to press his fingers against the portrait's glass, against James's cheek, I went to his side. The least I could do was stand beside him while he grieved.

"Hi."

He looked startled; he had not heard me approach. An instant later his eyes were shadowed by guilt. "I'm sorry. I shouldn't be here."

"You're Brian," I said. "You of all people should be here. I'm glad you came. Thank you." The first genuine thanks I had given all day. Thank you, oh God thank you for being here, Brian, you don't know what it means.

I took him in my arms, held him to me as insistently as he held me, as if we may be lost, swept under a fierce current, if either of us let go of this thing we both had known and shared.

9.

Brian announced his arrival with three sharp knocks on the door. X had fixed dinner for three and uncorked a bottle of red wine, the first wine I had ever tasted. It was bitter and tangy, as forceful as a psalm on my tongue. I answered the door to the house on the Bench and offered Brian his own glass, a water tumbler half-full of garnet-red wine. He smiled on the threshold. His smile was kind and boyish, sweet, with crooked canine teeth that gave him a look of mischief. James had loved this man. James had loved this smile. I led Brian inside.

Over dinner we did not talk of James. It was still too near and cutting, our loss. Instead X cheered us with stories of the strangest illustrations he had ever been hired to create. Brian and I both laughed louder and longer than we might have under other circumstances, but it was not forced. Laughter in the midst of grief feels like surfacing after a long dive. X played butler and entertainer, serving us both, binding us together with wine and good food, drawing in his quicksilver way permanent lines between us. Throughout the evening, Brian often paused to look around the house, taking in the angles and shadows of the place where James had lived, this plot where the man he loved had staked out his life and toiled.

"I'm going to put the house up for sale," I told him. It seemed important, that he should know that I would not remain, that I, like him, would carry James's memory away from this place.

"Where will you go?"

X and I looked at each other over our tumblers of wine. "I'm going to Seattle." "Maybe it's time for me to go somewhere else, too," Brian said. "Idaho Falls is too small for me now."

"You ought to take a road trip," X said. "It does wonders for your perspective."

I told Brian of the things I had seen on our drive through the West, the redness of the desert, the shape of tracks in sand. X left us talking on the sofa while he cleared away our dishes. At last he beckoned Brian into the kitchen with a discreet sideways jerk of his head. I swirled the last of the wine in my tumbler, watched the moon travel over the valley. X and Brian held a brief whispered conversation, heads down, man to man, and when it concluded they shook hands in a businesslike way, slapped each other on the shoulders, and Brian's face was flushed. He turned from X with brimming eyes. I pointed him in the direction of the bathroom.

Veil

X watched me from the kitchen, leaning one hip against the counter. I remembered the time I had kissed him there – apples – and to my relief the memory brought no guilt with it. I went to him. I leaned my forehead against his warm, welcome shoulder. Framed by the kitchen window, a spray of stars clamored in the late summer sky.

"I gave him the portrait," X whispered.

"I love you."

Brian cleared his throat. X and I broke away from each other to play host and hostess once more. Brian said he ought to be going, ought to get some sleep; he had to drive home in the morning.

"Stay here tonight, if you want to, if it's not too hard on you."

He thought about it a moment. "I'd like that. Thank you."

"We'll all sleep here, right here on the living room floor. There are air mattresses in the garage.

We've got plenty of blankets. I don't want you to be alone."

"I appreciate it."

"There's more wine," X said.

Baptism for the Dead

"Good."

The stars brightened the lace curtains in the window. They glowed – energy and matter. The smallest parts of everything I loved about you, James, motes, indestructible, drifting all through this place, in the air between Brian and me.

"It's nice outside," I said. "Let's go for a walk. Summer won't be here forever, and life is short." I led them across Poleline Road and into the potato field, the man who loved me and the man who loved my husband. The imperfect white blooms had all fallen away from the exhausted plants. The field was dark. Our feet turned the soil and stirred up the soft brown scent of potatoes ready for the harvest. I filled my lungs with the smell, breathing in more and more of it until my chest ached.

"Look at all the stars," I said, and took X and Brian by their hands. I thought in Brian's palm I could still feel the touch of James's own fingers. And in X's hand, I could feel the memory of the portrait that had made James live on.

What we could not do for you in life, James, we will do for you now. We who have passed through the refiner's fire – we who saw you and loved you – we will take you in our hands, take you in our arms and hold your memory against

Veil

our hearts. We will fall with you through the veil into a black ocean, and together we will rise up, whole and clean. You have gone into the earth, into the harvest, into the endless cycle of white flowers blanketing the Bench. You are the shadow of the water tower. You are an R over my heart. You are sunrise, and birds in bounding flight over prairies of sage. You are a great flock of black birds twisting in the air, and the sound of their wings can drown out even the voice of God.

*

That night I rose up long after the crickets had ceased their chorus. I was in the grip of a waking dream, or perhaps I did not dream at all. I stood in the living room of the house on the Bench, and to the left and right of me Brian and X lay sprawled in sleep, breathing slow.

I heard a voice in the kitchen. I followed it. Like a spirit, the breath of a whisper led me through the darkness to the mud room, to the garage door, across the cold cement floor that smelled faintly of gasoline and mildew. It led me out into the front yard where the crab apple tree stood still under the starred sky.

There was movement at the tree's roots.

Baptism for the Dead

Two points of purple shimmered and blinked. The voice drew me closer.

Under the tree was the small black shape of a dog crouching on its haunches. It wagged its tail.

Hello, I said. I know you.

The bare bones of its face grinned at me. Its eyes were violet lights, living and deep. When it opened its sharp-toothed mouth a multitude of voices spoke at once. James's voice, and X's, mine and Katherine's, my father's, and more, voices I had never heard before.

And so you are going away.

I am.

The dog turned its purple eyes to the car, X's hybrid slumbering in the driveway. I got into the driver's seat. The window was down. The dog put its paws up against the door where its nails clicked in a timid rhythm, the sound of Marlee tapping at the window. When I reached down to untie the bailing twine from the dog's neck I felt a collar, silvery and dull, chilling my fingers. I explored it with my hands, felt the badge shape with its heroic letters. I let the twine fall.

Thank you, said the dog in its thousand voices.

Veil

What do I do now? Now that I am going?

The dog laughed. It kicked the tire. A shower of sparks glittered across the yard, so bright they stung my eyes.

I told the dog, There is still an ember inside me. There is still a hot place where I can feel fear burning. I can feel the whole town burning there in my heart. I can't breathe through the smoke.

It seemed important that the dog should know. But it said nothing, only turned its white pointed face to gaze out across the valley.

I tried again: There is something small inside me, but it feels as if it might burst open at any moment and overwhelm me.

You swallowed your faith, the dog reminded me.

How do I put out the fire? Tell me.

The dog's mouth opened. Its thousand voices whispered together, murmuring, breathing. At last I made out their words.

Choose the right, they told me.

And I did.

*

Baptism for the Dead

In the morning I woke in the driver's seat of X's car. The window was up. I was very cold. I got out and stared around me, out into the field across Poleline Road where the three of us had walked the night before. A dark shadow slipped between the wilted plants, moving fast. An early frost lay on the potatoes, lacing the edges of the leaves. I glanced down at my feet, but there was no bailing twine lying in the drive. Of course there was none.

Down in the valley a dust devil swayed. The sun was sweet on Our Mountain.

The summer was over.

I went inside to pack my things.

ABOUT THE AUTHOR

Libbie Hawker writes historical and literary fiction featuring complex characters and rich details of time and place.

Originally from Rexburg, Idaho, she now lives in the San Juan Islands of Washington State with her husband, Paul.

Find more information at LibbieHawker.com

Made in the USA
Middletown, DE
01 February 2020